'Packs one hell of a punch … *Peach* inhabits a strange, horror-story realm of the hyperreal, and Glass's vision goes a long way towards portraying an experience that's near-impossible to articulate' Lucy Scholes, *Observer*

'Emma Glass's *Peach* begins with a young woman staggering home after a violent sexual attack and explores, in poetic language, the fallout from that catastrophe' *Sunday Times*

'Addressing an all-too-relevant issue, the novel charts the physical and psychological effects on Peach through stylised, poetic prose' *Independent*, Books to look out for in 2018

'A visceral work' *New Statesman*

'The dark poetic world of Emma Glass's debut, *Peach*, immerses the reader in a young woman's personal hell … Through prose that is lyrical, mythic and yet wonderfully clear, *Peach* expounds on themes of good versus evil, and the base nature of desire, consumption and carnality' *Irish Times*

'You won't be able to stop reading this visceral, unputdownable read … It's about good and evil, violence and redemption. But it is also a book that explores the beauty of language. Lyrically and visually driven, it's no wonder Glass's influences include James Joyce, Gertrude Stein and Kate Bush – her sentences read like powerful poems. Her words so emotive, you'll need to take a moment to catch your breath' *Elle*

'A book to be devoured in a single sitting … Glass is an exciting new author to know' *Vogue*

'A gutsy, discomfiting experiment' *Metro*

'A truly original voice for the future' *Big Issue*

'Dramatizes the ways powerful emotions evaded or repressed make themselves powerfully felt … Sinister and vivid' *Literary Review*

'Impossible to categorise, intimately weird and exhilaratingly bold, *Peach* shares literary DNA with Gertude Stein, Hubert Selby Jr, and Eimear McBride, but Emma Glass's massive talent is all her own' Laline Paull, author of *The Bees*

'*Peach* is a work of genius. So lonesome and moving, so gruesome, wry, tender and plaintive. It is the new *Jane Eyre*, and one wild, thrilling ride. Swallow it in one gulp, and carry a spare copy in your pocket. Always' Lucy Ellmann

'*Peach* is ferocious, startling, all-consuming … It has changed the way I see the world' Daisy Johnson

'What it lacks in pages (*Peach* has just 98), it makes up for in uniqueness' *Red*, Most Hotly Anticipated Books of 2018

'A propulsive, unforgettable read that's impossible to shake' *Entertainment Weekly*

EMMA GLASS was born in Swansea. She studied English Literature and Creative Writing at the University of Kent, then decided to become a nurse and went back to study Children's Nursing at Swansea University. She is a clinical research nurse and lives in North London. *Peach* is her first book.

@Emmas_Window

EMMA GLASS

PEACH

BLOOMSBURY PUBLISHING
LONDON · OXFORD · NEW YORK · NEW DELHI · SYDNEY

BLOOMSBURY PUBLISHING
Bloomsbury Publishing Plc
50 Bedford Square, London, WC1B 3DP, UK

BLOOMSBURY, BLOOMSBURY PUBLISHING and the Diana logo are
trademarks of Bloomsbury Publishing Plc

First published in Great Britain 2018
This edition published 2019

A catalogue record for this book is available from the British Library.

ISBN: HB: 978-1-4088-8669-4; Ebook: 978-1-4088-8667-0
PB: 978-1-4088-8651-9

2 4 6 8 10 9 7 5 3 1

Typeset by Integra Software Services Pvt. Ltd.
Printed and bound in Great Britain by CPI Group (UK) Ltd, Croydon CR0 4YY

To find out more about our authors and books visit www.bloomsbury.com and
sign up for our newsletters

For my family

Seam Stress

Thick stick sticky sticking wet ragged wool winding round the wounds, stitching the sliced skin together as I walk, scraping my mittened hand against the wall. Rough red bricks ripping the wool. Ripping the skin. Rough red skin. Rough red head. I pull the fuzzy mitten from my fingers, wincing as the torn threads grip the grazes on my knuckles. It is dark. The blood is black. Dry. Crack crackly crackling. The smell of burnt fat clogs my nostrils. I put my fingers to my face and wipe the grease away. It clings to my tongue, crawls in my mouth, sliding over my teeth, my cheeks, dripping down my throat. I am sick. The sick is pink in the moonlight. Fleshy. Fatty. I lean against the wall and close my eyes. I swallow hard. I taste flesh. Meat. I am sick again. My eyes flicker. Flashes of pink. Back to black. My body buzzes against the bricks. I see black. Thick black. Fat. My eyelids are fat. Swollen. Swollen black from the slap. Smothered in grease from his slippery slimy sausage fingers. His commands crackle in my ears. Close your eyes. Close them tight. Tight like your—close them. Close them. Close them.

I see black. His black mouth. A slit in his skin. Open. Gaping. Burnt black. Burnt flesh. And his heavy charcoal breath clinging to my skin. Suffocating. The tears slide over the grease and off my face. My body buzzes. I need to go home but it hurts when I walk. I put my hand between my legs and feel the blood and grease. I am sick. I wipe my mouth on my sleeve, put my mitten in my mouth and grind the wool between my teeth. I run. Not far. Not fast. It hurts too much. I grind the wool harder. I wish it was steel. I look back. Sick runs in ribbons after me. Shimmering pink rivers. I hope it rains.

I slip inside. I don't open the door wide. It still squeaks. They will hear. They will corner me in the hall. They will ask me questions. He won't ask about the blood. She won't ask about the rips in my clothes. She will say the rose in my cheeks looks pretty. He will kiss my head and say dinner is at seven. I swallow a mouthful of sick and slip silently up the stairs still chewing my mitten.

In the bathroom I switch on the shower and stand under it. I don't take off my clothes. The warm water stings. Tingles my skin. I grip my lip with my teeth. My clothes cling to my skin and it sting sting stings as I strip. I fling them. Fat fabric. Saturated with blood and grease and water. They flap against the bath and flop to the floor. The water runs red. Black and red. Mostly red. I wash slowly. With my fingers. Lots of soap. So much soap. I rub. It hurts. Through the suds I watch my tears drown, fall down the drain. I want to follow and fall with them. Drown. Slip down. In the warm. In the dark. I sit in the tub. Put in the plug. I close my eyes.

I open my eyes when the water fills my nostrils. I wrap my toes around the chain and tug until the plug pops and stops stopping the water from filling the tub to the top. I watch the pools of grease floating on the water. White. Whirling. Floating. Slowly. Unashamedly. Enjoying the water. My water. I allow my aching face to smile slightly when they get sucked suddenly down the hole. Not my hole.

It takes a long time for me to stand. My swollen legs won't bend. I hold on to the side of the tub and ease my body out of the water. My bones crunch. I scrunch my face, squeeze my eyes shut, press my lips together so the screams don't escape. I stand under the shower and start to scrub. The water is cold now. I don't care. I need to be clean. I need to rub the red from my skin. Scrub the grease away. The soap slips off. Cold. The drips prick my skin, push through, rush through, collide with my bones. Red blood runs to blue. Buzzing bones stand still. Cold. Numb. I switch off the shower. Reach for the towel. Step out of the shower. The towel doesn't feel fluffy against my skin. Doesn't feel warm. Doesn't feel. I don't feel.

I walk along the hall silently. Open the door to my room silently. Close the door to my room silently. But it's too late. They hear. They storm up the stairs. Trample each other. Twist around the banister. There is no lock on the door. I lean against it. They hurl their bodies against the frame. The door flicks open and I fly. Hit the wall. The towel drops. Four eyes. Big. Blue. Glassy. Open. Wide. Staring. Mam pushes Dad out of the room. Shuts the door. He coughs. Sorry, Peach, he says. You should have said. Go downstairs please, Dad, says Mam. We hear him step softly down the stairs. I pull the towel round me and sit on the bed. Mam sits down next to me. You snuck upstairs sneakily, says Mam. We didn't even hear you come in. Her eyes are big and glassy and I can see my puny bare shoulders reflected in her pulsating pupils. Her eyes are rolling over my face and my body and she is smiling. Her smile is pink and takes up most of her face. I came in quietly because I didn't want to wake up Baby. I thought he might have been sleeping, I say. Oh you're a good girl, Peach, she says. He's only just fallen asleep. Good girl. She strokes my wet hair. What do you want for dinner? she says. I'm not hungry, Mam, I say, looking down. Oh don't be silly. I was going to do pasta and meatballs for me and Dad. Shall I do you the same and put vegetables in the sauce instead? I've got some lovely baby sweet-corns there. She smacks her lips and nods and her eyes bounce around in her head. I'm all right, Mam, honest. I look up to see if she has noticed the puddle of red between my legs that is saturating the towel. Splat. Splattering on the carpet. She blinks in sync with the drips. Right, well I'll do it for you just in case you're hungry after. She kisses the top of my head. You're looking a bit peaky, Peach. She pinches my cheeks with her beaky fingers. She stands up and scuttles out of the room. She turns back and smiles at me before she shuts the door. Her lips look like the meat I threw up earlier.

I take the mirror from the shelf. I spread the towel on the floor and sit with my back against the door. I part my legs slowly and slot the mirror between my thighs. I put my hand over my mouth to stop the sick. I use my other hand to touch. The skin is split. Slit. Sliced. With two trembling fingers I touch the split skin, hold the slit together. Blood dribbles delicately. I look closely into the mirror. Fluid streams from my eyes, trickles over my tummy, runs into the red. Little rivers. Little ribbons. Slithers of silk. Torn skin. Stained scarlet. I need to stop the bleeding. I lean forward and wrap my hands around the leg of the desk in front of me and pull myself up. I pull a tissue from the box on the desk and place it between my legs. I put on my dressing gown. Slip on my slippers. Slide down the stairs. Mam is in the kitchen. Cooking. I smell the meat. Beef. Burning. His breath is in my nostrils. Sharp smoke. Suffocating. I swallow.

Aren't you dressed yet? says Mam. No. I have to sew up a hole in my jeans, I say. That scabby pair? Just chuck them in the bin, Peach. We'll go into town and get you some new ones this week. She pinches my bum as I move past her. I open the cupboard under the sink and take out the sewing basket. I've got some other things to sew too, I say. She makes a clicking noise with her tongue, licks the sauce off the spoon. I slide past and run up the stairs. I forgot the ice. I scramble back down the stairs. I fumble in the freezer, find the ice tray. Too much movement. Blood dribbles down my leg. Mam doesn't see. Sid stalks in. The padding of his paws on the floor silences the splattering. He winds his body around my legs. His fur feels soft. His fur stains red. I untangle my legs from his fuzzy body and leave him lapping up the splatters.

I close the door to my room and lean against it. I look around. I don't know what I'm looking for. I pick the towel up and spread it again in the same spot. I take the soggy tissue from between my legs and put it in the bin. I search the sewing box for pink- or peach-coloured thread. I don't find any. I use white. I thread it through a needle. It takes a long time. My fingers are still shaking. I knot twice. Three times. Four. That is enough. I hit the ice tray against the desk. Hard. The cubes bounce out. Three fit in my mouth. I sit on the towel. Open my legs. Position the mirror. Oh. I take a cube of ice and press it to my skin. Oh. Cold. Oh. I slide it down over my—cold. So oh cold. I push the ice against the slice. Hold it there. Water drips off my fingers. The cold is soothing. I wait till the ice is melted. The ice is still solid in my mouth. In the mirror my lips look swollen and blue. Puffed up. Rock hard. They look like they will fall off my face. I look down. Oh. The slit is smaller. Still split. I take the needle. I hold the cold skin together with two fingers. Tug the thread. Suck the ice. Point the needle. Push it in. Stop. Scratch. Scratching. Cat. Not now. Scratch. Not now, Sid. Scratching. I want him to go away. Scratching stops. I wait. He has gone. I start. Slip the pin through the skin. Start stitching. It doesn't sting. It does bleed. White thread turns red. Red string. Going in. Going out. I pull. Tug. Tug the pin. In. Out. Out. Out. Blackout.

Peach! The screech forces my eyes open. Peach! Dinner is ready! Come down please. Mam is standing at the bottom of the stairs. I hear Dad scuttle into the kitchen, scraping his chair on the tiles, sitting down. I reach for scissors. Snip. The bleeding has stopped. I look around the room. I am looking for clothes. I find pyjamas. They will ask why, I will say I am sleepy. I fold up the towel and stuff it in the bin. I will put the sewing basket back later.

I open the kitchen door and peer in. They grin manically at me. Big eyes. Big. Staring. I struggle to smile. I sit down next to Dad. On the plate, in front of me, vegetables. Green and yellow. Pasta. Light yellow. Colours. Not pink. I am hungry. Looks good, I say to Mam. She smiles. She watches. She wants to see me eat. So I eat. Slowly. I cut up the corn. Cut up the beans. Twist the pasta around the fork. Twirling. And in. I chew. Dad shovels the spaghetti into his smile. I can't smell their meat. We eat. I am full. I drink water. I can feel it lay flat on the food in my tummy. It swishes and swirls in my stomach when I stand up and move to the other room. Baby is asleep, says Mam. Be quiet. I open the door quietly, gently. The lights are low, they glow. Warm yellow. The cot is in the corner. Baby is sitting up. Smiling at me. Big smile. Bigger than Mam and Dad's. He holds on to the bars with wobbly arms. He giggles, his skin wiggles as I move closer, smiling. I feel my face with my fingers. Curved lips. Smile. I am smiling. I stretch out my arms to Baby. He tries to pull himself up but he has jelly legs. He wobbles and topples over. His cry flies through the air and pricks open my heart. I scoop him up out of the cot, hold him close to my chest. Kiss his head. Lick the icing sugar off my lips. His red face looks redder in the low light. I sway slowly side to side until his cries subside. I tickle his wiggling cheeks. His open mouth

8

closes and slips back into a smile. I move with him to the sofa and sit. It is warm in front of the fire. He glows. Hi Baby, I say, soothingly. His back sticks to my skin where the icing sugar has rubbed away. His body vibrates in my arms. Wiggling skin. Sticky. Jelly. Jelly Baby. Baby. He gurgles. I tickle his jelly tummy. I can see my arm through his transparent body. I shift his weight. Remove my arm from his back. Lay him on my lap. My arm feels warm. I rub the red gum from it. Baby is melting. I am such an idiot. I pick him up and take him to the table. I sit him on the mat, put pillows behind his back, reach for the icing-sugar shaker. The mat sticks to his back when I try to turn him over. I peel him from the plastic. His lips wobble. He is going to cry. Shush, Baby, shush. Shush, Baby, I say. I smooth his back. Shape the jelly. Sprinkle him with sugar. Shush. Peach is silly, I say, isn't she? Isn't Peach silly? He giggles and gurgles. I am still smiling. I still sprinkle. I lift him up off the mat and watch the excess sugar slip off him. I swing him around and he giggles. Good as new. Mam and Dad swing the door open. They stand and stare. Their smiles grow simultaneously. They scamper in and sit down, side by side. They hold hands. I hold Baby close to my chest and bounce his body gently. His jelly body jiggles. See? says Dad. He just takes some getting used to, that's all. We know he came as a bit of a surprise to you, Peach, says Mam. But a baby brother will be good

for you. I bounce Baby. I look at Mam. Her eyes are
so big. So blue. Her tummy pokes out over her trou-
sers. Just a bit. She is losing her pregnancy weight.
She has been having sex. She sees me looking, pulls
her sweater down. Sticks her tongue out at me. Dad
grins. It'll be good practice, he says. For what? I can
feel my forehead crease. For when you and Green
have babies. For when we what? I say. I stop bounc-
ing Baby. Now, Peach, we know what is going on.
We are your parents. We weren't born yesterday. We
know you two have been – you know, says Dad. Baby
wriggles in my arms. I hand him to Mam. No, Dad. I
don't think I do know. I'm too young to have babies,
I say, slouching in the chair by the fire. But Baby will
have someone to play with! Mam jumps forward,
nearly dropping Baby. Dad's head bobs up and down
excitedly. Go on, says Mam. Green is a lovely boy.
You make such a cute couple. And the sex sounds
amazing, says Dad. My face flickers red like Baby's.
I can't see it. But I feel hot. I turn my face to the fire.
I burn with it. Mam giggles and pinches Dad's cheek.
It's okay, Peach. Sex is a good thing. Me and Mam
do it all the time. We just did it now on the kitchen
table. It's human nature, Peach, don't be embarrassed.
Green is a lucky guy. Most girls won't put out until
they are married. But not our Peach. And we're proud
of you. It is good to get experience, and well, if you
get blessed with a baby, that's even better. I cover my

face with my hands. I want to cry. That Green looks like he's a big boy. I bet you have a brilliant time, says Mam. Her tongue is still hanging out of her mouth when I look at her through parted fingers. She turns her head and sticks her tongue in Dad's mouth. I can't watch this. I take Baby from Mam, kiss him on the head and put him back in his cot. He sits there wriggling and giggling, watching Mam and Dad roll around on the sofa. Kissing. Biting. Eyes wide. Mam gives me a little wave. I can't watch this. I leave the room quickly. Quietly. Up the stairs. Close the door to my room. Flop down on the bed. Exhausted.

I lie with my hand on my stomach. It feels swollen. Full. I close my eyes and think of Green. My gorgeous Green. I wish he was here. Lying next to me. With his hand on my stomach. His lips on my neck. I feel full. So full. I ate too much. Must have eaten too much. I think of the food as a foetus. What would I do? Peach and Green. With a baby. Mam and Dad would be ecstatic. Baby would have someone to play with. Baby will have someone to play with anyway if Mam and Dad don't stop sexing every six seconds. I'm too young to have a baby. Green would leave me. No he wouldn't. But he would be scared. I would be scared. I nearly melted my brother. If my baby was jelly too it wouldn't stand a chance.

I like this full feeling. I rub my tummy. Full. Firm. I open the buttons of my shirt, flip back the flannel.

Lines of orange light lie on my skin from the street lamp. I follow the lines with my fingers. Strange shadows break the lines of light. Swinging over my skin. Orange. Broken with black. Swings back to orange. I sit up. Orange flashes around the room. I walk to the window. I have to hold on to the sill to steady myself when I see him swinging from the street light. Holding on to the lamp with his slimy sausage fingers. Swinging. Sausages dangling. *I have to close my eyes. I have to open my eyes.* His long, thick body bobbing back and forth. Back. And. Forth. Swing. Swinging sausages. Swinging cylinder arms. *I have to blink hard.* Thick. Fat. His mouth is open. I can see the smoke spilling from the slit in his skin. In his face. His face. He doesn't have a face. Holes pricked in the skin of the top end of his body, sort of body, where his face should be. Deep holes. Black. And a bit further down a smouldering slit. *I have to grip the windowsill.* I am scared. *I rub my eyes. I see him.* He is swinging from the street light. He is waving to me with his sausage arm. Wiggling his sausage fingers. Greasy glistening skin in the orange light. Long sausage legs slipping over the pavement. Thick. Fat. Swing. Swinging. Swing. Ing.

Break Fast

Rays reach through the window and pry my eyes open. I close them. Light leaks through the lids. They lift. I am lying on the floor, looking up at the ceiling. My head hurts. My neck hurts. My cheek is wet with little licks from Sid's pink tongue. He purrs and pads with his little paws, clawing the carpet, licking and looking into my face. I stroke his head and sit up. My tummy doubles under my breasts and I reach down and rub the rolls. They feel like sausages stretched over my stomach. Swollen. Sore. Still. I stand. Sid skims my shins and jumps up and sits on the windowsill. Last night lies before me. A picture, framed perfectly by unclosed curtains. The dark sky, the swinging sausage man. I close the curtains quickly. Sunlight shines through. I feel silly. I open them. The sky is blue, light, it's not night. I am silly. There is no sausage man. I turn away and stretch. My bones click. I pause in that position. I stretch my arms above my head and look down at my stomach sticking out. I shrug. Time to put on clothes for college. I open the cupboard and pull out jeans. The baggy pair that need a belt. Pull off pyjamas, reach for panties, put them on. Socks first. My toes are cold. Jeans next. Pull them up. Button up. They won't button up. I breathe in. They are usually too big, I usually need a belt. I breathe in again and force the fly. It zips up. But it didn't want to. My tummy pushes over the sides. I reach for a sweater that will swamp my skin, hide my sagging stomach. I look at my slumped figure in the mirror. I wrinkle my nose. Disgust. It will do. I brush through my blonde bushy hair, bushy from when I slept with it wet and it fizzes and is fuzzy so I tie it up high on my head. In a knot. I tie a ribbon too so it looks like I tried.

Toothbrush time. Brushing-teeth trauma. There is a mirror above the sink with a little light and an orange bulb that makes everything look pink. I clutch the brush and squirt the paste from the tube and place the bristles on my tongue and taste the paste. The paste tastes of mint. I rub it into my tongue and it tingles. Scrubbing and splashing water. I splash water in my mouth and watch the white-forming foam spill out, looking pink in the light, light pink, not quite white. I make a grin and bare my teeth to see if they are clean but they look pink and are covered in paste so I splash more water and then they shine. I close my mouth and splash water on my face and press the dark patches under my eyes. Peach. More like Patch. Even in the light my skin is grey with no glow. No glow. I need to go. I lift the lid and unzip the jeans, pull down the panties and sit down on the pan. The water passes. Pain. Sting. I bite my lip to keep the cry in. And when I wipe there is blood. I zip up and flush. Stand and steady myself, gripping the basin with both hands. I twist the tap and run the water, close my eyes and splash my face. I should forget. I will forget. I pinch my cheeks and sigh. I will try.

Peach, there is a letter for you, says Dad. How exciting. I sip some orange juice and hold out my hand. Dad pulls my thumb then puts the letter in my palm. Love letter, is it? He winks at me. I roll my eyes and drink more juice. Let me get the letter opener, he says. No it's okay, I say, slipping my thumb under the seal. He flips my thumb out of the way and slices open the envelope with his bronze blade. There we go. I pull the paper out. A single sheet. I unfold. It is slimy. I unfold. Again. I spread it out on the table and push the creases. My fingers feel oily. I put them to my nose. Smell. Meat. They smell like sausage. I look at the sheet. Newspaper words, cut out. I fold it in half quickly so Mam and Dad don't see. Dad is spooning sugar into Baby's mouth. He is gurgling. Sitting in his high chair, wiggling his little legs. Enjoying. Mam is munching toast and reading the newspaper. I fold up the letter and place it in my pocket. I drink up the rest of my juice. I'm going now, I say. Hang on, says Dad. What was in that letter? Oh, it's just Green, being a goof, I say. I smile. Dad moves over to Mam and kisses her on the cheek. Remember the time I wrote you a letter? he asks. Mam looks up at him and smiles. She nods and puckers her lips. She pouts until he kisses her. It drives me wild when you do that, he says, moving his mouth down and kissing her neck. I'm going, I say again, swiping the envelope, slipping it in my backpack, slinging it on my shoulder, sliding over to Baby, kissing his jelly head, licking the sugar off my lips, leaving through the open door.

I drop my backpack on the drive, put my coat on. It's cold. I reach in my pockets for my mittens but they're not there. I shrug into my backpack and stuff my hands in my pockets. I find the paper and pull it out. The grease glistens in the sunlight and I hold it up to see better. Newspaper words cut out. Stuck on. With. I sniff. Slime. Sausage. Oil. It smells. Strong. And it says:

Peach. Don't run away from me again. Love, Lincoln.

Love. Lincoln. Lincoln. He has a name. And he has love. I fold the paper in two, in four, put it in my pocket and wonder how he managed to use scissors with his fat sadistic sausage fingers. I shudder and shake his shadow from my shoulders. I will focus and forget and think about Green.

Sun Screen

I sit in the sun and look up at the sky and count the clouds. One is a wolf. Two is a toad. Three is a tree. Four. My eyes are sore from staring. I look down at the grey ground. A shadow stops the sun from shining on my face. His twig-thin fingers touch my cheek. They smell like cigarettes and springtime. I take shade under his chest and bury my face in his brown sweater. I suck in the scent of limes and wet leaves. I lift my head and touch my lips to his wooden smile. It cracks into a kiss. I let the stubble on his chin splinter my skin. I shaved today and everything, he says, his damp lips still kissing. And everything, I repeat, kissing his cheek, pulling him down to sit on the seat. I sit and slide my fingers between his. He snaps his hand around mine and I feel safe. I rest my head against his arm. I can't reach his shoulder. Sleepy, sweet Peach? he asks. The soft sounds grow out of his thick throat, fall from his mouth and float down. I hear them as they fall. Yes, I say. And another long day before I can go to sleep again. I let out a little yawn. Green gazes down at the grazes on my knuckles. His smile buckles. You're hurt, he says. I run my fingers over the dry blood. I should tell him. I fell down. Last night. In the dark, I say. He kisses the cuts. I'm sorry I wasn't with you. I should tell him. You didn't phone me when you got home, either. He kisses my mouth and I taste twigs. His brown eyes take root in mine. Sorry—I stutter. I was worried, he says. My heart hits my ribcage. Hard. I hope he doesn't hear it. I was worried. I wish I could tell him. I shouldn't have let you walk home alone so late. Too late. It's okay. Why didn't you phone? he asks. I stutter. I splutter. Sick crawls up my throat. I pull the collar of my coat tight around my neck and swallow. My heart batters my lungs and my breath bursts out in little bullets. I want to tell him. I was taking care of Baby. Weak words. They don't reach his ears. I look up at the light filtering through his hair. Warm brown shadows fall across his face and I kiss the creases they make. Did you grow taller? I ask. He clutches my chin with his thin fingers. They feel smooth, breakable. Not thick. Not fat. Not solid. Not sausages. I shudder. What's wrong? I sigh. I smile. He searches my eyes. I'm fine. You are taller, I say. He shrugs. He smiles. Just don't get too high or you'll leave the ground. I won't do that, he says. Not while you're around. His arm branches out behind my back and he tangles himself around me. I suck in his scent. I want to stay this way. Sleep with me tonight, he says. I smile. It's cold, let's go inside.

Where is Sandy? says Green. I shrug. Are we early? It's not like him not to be waiting for you. His knees creak as we walk along the corridor. Poor little love-sick puppy. His laugh echoes deep in his throat. He isn't lovesick, I say. We are friends. His fingers tangle my hair as he stoops to walk through the doorway. I know he says, smiling. He twirls me around to face him. I frown, just friends. He kisses my head. Are you swimming today? No, I say. Okay. We can walk home together. I nod and drop his hand. He touches my tummy. See you after. I watch him leave. His hand donates a damp peat print to my stomach. I put my hand in its place and press. Firm. Fat. I frown. I look down. Can't see my shoes.

Silver coins in the slot. Hot coffee to warm my frozen fingers. I need new mittens. Push the swing door open, hear it swoosh shut. I slip off my back-pack and put it on the blue plastic table and sit on the blue plastic chair attached to it. I shiver, staring down at the brown coffee currents in the cup. I dip a finger in the thin liquid. It burns and turns my finger red and I take it out and put it in my mouth. Swoosh. In swings Hair Netty. I look up, still suck-ing my finger. She smooths my head with her hairy hand and sits in the chair opposite me. Don't stare. Don't stare at her hair. Don't stare at her hair, I tell myself. I politely pretend not to notice when thick black strands fall into the cup and soak up the coffee. Well isn't it quiet in here today? she squeaks. I can't see her mouth because her moustache has grown so long over her lips, but her big blue eyes smile out at me through black strands. Yes, I say. It's quiet today. I hadn't noticed. I look around. The plastic chairs attached to the plastic tables are all empty and I am glad because I want to be alone. You are quiet too, squeaks Hair Netty. Her hairy hands hold back the strands covering her face and for a moment her nose shows. She stuffs the hairs under the net on her head. Instantly they escape. She sighs. It's no good. It's just no good, she squeaks. I try to make my smile look like it means sympathy. Any news? she squeaks. Not really, I say, I just have biology class today. She is struggling with the strands so she smooths her apron instead. Up and down. Up and down the white stripes. Just one class. So you won't be around for lunch, she squeaks. No, I say, what lovely lunch am I missing out on? She smiles and squeaks, Sausage and mash. My heart works harder but my face refuses to fill with blood. My goodness! squeaks Hair Netty. You look sick Peach, what's wrong? Sausage and mash is everyone's favourite. I feel faint. I'm going to faint. Oh silly me! I forgot. You're vegetarian, aren't you? She strokes my arm with her hairy hand. That's right, I say shakily, hoping my face soon stops being white.

She chuckles squeakily, her hair swishing from side to side. It shines in the light. She must use conditioner. Or olive oil. Just as well then, can't have you swallowing sausages if you don't like them, she squeaks. I swallow a mouthful of sick. Well, Peach, I must get on. Potatoes won't peel themselves. She gathers up her hair and swings it over her shoulder. See you soon, she squeaks, scuttling into the kitchen.

Must have sucked all the air out of the room because I don't breathe any more in. I go to the window and twist the latch and scratch, the frame scratches as I lift the pane up. I place my face in the open air and breathe in, breathe in. The breath I breathe out freezes to fog and floats away. The day has turned grey. The wolf must have eaten the toad and sat under the tree because now the clouds are one and wider than my eyes can see. Going grey because the day is older. I don't mind. I'd like this day to be. Over. Cold air catches in my nose, numbs my nostrils, fills my pharynx with frost. And, oh. In goes the air that clings to the hairs in my nose, the air freezing in my throat, the air that makes me choke. Choke. The smell. The. Smell. Of. Smoke. Barbecued pork. I smell pork. Pork smoke forking my nose, filling my throat. I choke. I choke. I choke. He is here. I look for Lincoln out of the window. But I can't see him. But I can see thick drying fat on the black tarmac. Slime like a slug leaves. Like a slug. I think about salt.

If I threw salt on a slug it would dissolve and die. If I threw salt on a sausage it would taste better.

I try to shut the window but it catches. I pull the letter from Lincoln out of my pocket. I read it once through then tear it up and throw it in the bin. I tear up the envelope too and put it in the bin. He knows my name. I put my backpack on my back and walk to the biology lab. He knows where I live. He delivered the letter himself. I keep close to the wall as I walk along the corridor. I walk and it feels like I walk for miles. I look down at the floor tiles. Lines of tiles. Linking tiles. Links of sausages. Links of Lincolns. Each black line is the slit of his chargrilled smile. Miles of smiles. Grills and grins and sausages going in. Going in. Sting. It stings. I need to sit. My thighs don't feel like they can balance the weight of my swelling belly any more. I wait by the wall for a minute. My hands move from my sides to my stomach and it feels tight and round. I roll on and reach the lab and I am glad to sit down.

Brain Freeze

Smells sweet. Smells like soft hot sugar steaming in a saucepan on a stove. Smells sweet so I sit up straight and suck it in. Clattering chairs. Legs scatter. Sandy slips into the seat next to mine. I glance and send him a small smile sideways. Hi Peach, says Sandy. His hand waves and he grabs my smile and puts it in his pocket. He smiles and piles his books on the desk. He squares the stack and leans back in his chair. I smell him, but I don't see him, he says, grinning. He slipped in for a few seconds, I say. I think he went to get coffee. Oh. So, we can expect some super spillage, says Sandy, still smiling. I nod and sigh and look away from Sandy to the window. Looks like snow. It looks like it's going to snow, Sandy. I don't think it's cold enough. He snaps his neck to the side and stares and smiles. You know, Peach, I've been trying to reach you all weekend, he says. I've been busy, Sandy, I say, still looking away. I can feel his eyes still staring at me. I turn to him and he looks down at the desk. His smile shrinks. I wanted to ask—

Hi class, says Mr Custard, his thick voice spills through the doorway, followed by his blobby body. Sandy's speech gets cut off so he steals a look at my lips. I slip him another little smile. Or should I say, class half full! continues Mr Custard. He chuckles to himself, sets his cup of coffee down on the desk and rolls to the front of the room. We get smaller every week, he says, shaking his face, showering the first row with splatters of custard. Oops, he says. He sighs. Sorry. It's still early. I haven't quite set yet. His yellow cheeks shine scarlet. So we'll make a start. He sits on the side of the desk and slips directly on to the floor. This is not my morning. Laughter clutters in the corners of the room. I manage to giggle. Sandy, come here please, says Mr Custard. His voice is lower and thicker on the floor. He sounds like he needs to clear his throat. Help me up. I am stuck. Sandy stands slowly, balancing his big grin on his chin. He bends by Mr Custard's desk, and scoops the yellow goop up in his arms. That's it. Now if you can just stay there one moment while I gather myself. Sandy stays. He sways slightly, making little waves. We watch. Little ripples. Little rolls. That's it, says Mr Custard, keep swaying; if we get enough momentum, I can mould myself into a mound. Sandy sways. Custard curdles. Limbs form from liquid. Bits of arms, bits of legs, bits of bones but not really bones. Blobs. Brilliant yellow. Bold, now. Bubbling. Big, getting bigger. Sandy lets go and sits back down. We watch the waves rise up until Mr Custard is tall enough to almost touch the ceiling with the top of his soft, slowly forming cranium of custard skin.

Okay, we'll try again. So, today. The integumentary system. I can smell your excitement! Now, for those of you who don't have any skin, I promise you will still find this interesting, says Mr Custard. Now, take notes, we'll start with the epidermis.

I settle back in the seat, open my notebook, pull the lid off a pen and begin to listen. Stratified squamous, slow down so I can write it down. STRAT IF IED SQUA MOUS skin. Thin. Skin. Or is it thick? My skin is thin. I look at the scabs on my knuckles. Must have scratched them against the walls when I was— Sandy slips me a note that says, Are you okay? You seem distracted. I scribble in the space below his spider scrawl: I'm fine, thanks, I just don't like skin. And then he writes, But why not when yours is so beautiful and I blush because I am huge and hideous and he doesn't see it. Neither does Green. But Sandy is so – such a friend. I look away and out of the window. I see a shadow. No, not a shadow. It's far away. Near the fence. In the trees. As tall as them, and now shrinking beneath the bushes. It is brown. No, pink. And I'm shocked. And I'm not. No. That's not shock, because I know what it is, and now Mr Custard is calling me and my eyes are too wide open to cry and thank goodness because he wants me to answer a question and I don't think I can. If the window was open I would jump out of it.

Peach? I know you're not asleep because your eyes are open but you're not with us. Please pay attention. Skin accessories please, what are they? Oh, um, I fumble with my thumbs. I'm sorry, hairs and nails. That's right, and can you tell us what they're made of? Mr Custard stands close to our desk and drops a little blob in front of me. Keratin, I say. That's right, he says. I sigh inside. I'm so glad I read this chapter at the weekend. So you see, class, skin is a very unusual organ, it is made up of dead and alive cells. Half dead, half alive. But just like lucky little Peach here, although the skin we see is dead, hers looks very alive, very pretty – oh and now very pink! Sorry, we didn't mean to embarrass you! He chuckles and the class sends me sniggers through the air and they feel sharp in my back. I cover my face with my hands. I want to melt on the spot. My face feels hot. Can I open the window? I mumble without removing my hands. Yes, Peach, it is warm, and you don't look very well. Sandy jumps up and stretches over me and struggles with the latch. His shirt brushes my nose and it smells like salt. Grains of sand and salt shower me. Little sprinkles fall in my hair. Sorry, he says, sounding embarrassed. I don't mind. He slides the window up and the cold air covers my face and puts out the fire under my skin. Mr Custard looks at me. Oh my, he says and sees that the blood cells in my cheeks have risen to the surface and made shapes that spell the words SOMEONE HELP. His shining yellow eyes search my face. Peach, please stay after class, he says. I shut my eyes and wonder what I've given away.

Swear Blind

You haven't done anything wrong, says Mr Custard.
I have. My eyes drop to the desk. You're not in any
trouble, I just wanted to talk. I am. I am in trouble.
I'm in lots of pain and I'm very scared. You look
unwell, he says. He sits on the edge of the desk and
dents it. The legs creak and a crack streaks through
the surface of the wood but he doesn't look down.
His eyes steam into the back of my bare neck and
my skin feels warm like when I'm under the sun.
What's wrong, Peach? You can tell me. I look up.
I can't tell him. It's difficult to look at Mr Custard
when he is so close because he is bright yellow and
very shiny. I am considering sunglasses. He wants an
answer and I don't know what to say. I can't tell him.
Is something bothering you? I sit still, I don't shake
my head. I don't know what to do. I want to help
you, Peach, I know there is something wrong. My
head feels fuzzy like it did last night. I'm okay, I say
quietly. I look out the window. The sky looks full and

fuzzy, looks how I feel, looks like it will fall open and snow soon. I look further, for the sausage shadow, and find that Mr Custard has followed my gaze. His voice curdles and the separate sounds filter through the thick silence surrounding me. Peach? Are you looking for someone? Are you scared? I can't hear the sigh that escapes me but I'm sure he does. I look down again. I grip my thighs under the table. Sir— I almost tell him. I am scared, I say, slowly. The words slip, drip out. I wish they hadn't.

If you can't tell me, show me, he says. I pause then pick my heavy arm up and point to the window. Mr Custard stands and shifts himself to the window. He squints his sliding slits for eyes tight. They look closed to me but he has seen and he turns and says, I see. Don't worry, Peach, I will call security and they will escort him off the grounds. You're not walking home alone, are you? I shake my head and say no. How long has he been following you for? I shrug and shuffle to the door. Thank you, sir, I say.

Get me Green. Get me Green now. I feel faint I feel full I feel I'm falling down the stairs but I'm not, I'm flying, my feet take me far along the corridor to the cafeteria where we always meet. I fling my arms around him and the force of my weight makes him shake and sway. Hey, he says, what's wrong? I clutch him around the waist and say, Nothing, I just missed you today. He laughs and it echoes in the empty room. Shall we stroll? Slowly, I say. Outside now and I feel cool and calm because I am close to Green. We walk to the gates and through. I use my eyes to spy for shadows but see nothing. The sun is low and slowly slipping out of the sky. You shouldn't stare at the sun, says Green. I wasn't aware I had been staring but when I look up at Green and blink, the blotches of orange that cover his face don't go. The blotches blind me. I walk blind by Green's side. Blind side. Blindsided. And I close my eyes seeing as I can't see anyway. The orange blotches pin themselves to the inside of my eyelids. Pretty sun. Set. Scent. He's holding my hand but I follow his scent and the snapping sounds of his legs. Green is a good guide and when I open my eyes we're in the garden. Green bends and picks a flower from a bed. Not his bed. The flower is blue and he holds it to my face. Like the colour of your eyes, he says and ties it in my hair. I smile.

The moon has swapped with the sun and is climbing a silver string of stars to the centre of the sky. It will frost. It won't rain. But there are clouds and they cover the strange silver light. Strange because it's separate from the still-orange sky. Still orange. Still straining to change from orange to blue. How will it do that? Green shakes little leaves as he laughs. His laugh is deep and in his chest. His breath tickles his twiggy throat and makes deep, gentle notes. Pretty Peach, so fascinated by the sky. He pulls me in close from behind and tucks his long, thin fingers around my widening waist. It just happens so fast, I say in a sigh. Best not blink, he whispers close to my ears and it sounds so sweet I shut my eyes. Come inside, he says.

By the light of the fridge he fills two glasses with water. He's chewing on something that looks chewy. You sure you don't want some? I nod, not knowing what it is, don't want to know, not hungry, not thinking of food, thinking of full and feeling filled with wanting to watch. I want to watch without thinking. Want to see him bend. See him sway. He bends and sways and sends shadows soaring. It is beautiful. But I'm scared. It is dark in the kitchen and in the dim light his slender frame is making shadows like spiders. I am scared of spiders. Big, long, thin, crawling, creeping over the walls and floor, the room is full of slow, silent spiders. They swing from silver wisps of moonlight that cling to the window. A web. I am scared of spiders. I shudder. Green is oblivious to the friends that are fixed to his body, flinging themselves from him. I am shuddering, scared, but I can't close my eyes. I step back from the doorway. The shadow-spiders stretch their long legs into the hall, look like they will burst out of the frame, but then the fridge door is shut and the shadow-spiders scuttle away and Green steps out of the kitchen with the glasses of water in his hands, still chewing and smiling.

I stop shuddering as we go upstairs. Green leads, goes first, I follow. He doesn't switch on any lights. Never does. It's dark on the stairs. It's dark in his room. He closes the door. There are little bits of light leaking through the window. We sit on his bed and sink into the soft mattress side by side. He slides closer and bends to kiss my neck. He pulls at my soft wool sweater. He wants me to take it off. Look at him in the low light. His eyes are black like coal, charcoal — oh, no. No. Not like that. I can't compare his eyes to the thick black slits that stared and scarred and stole. I am relieved when he moves slightly and the last of the light gets caught in the lenses of his eyes. I forget and kiss him. He lifts the sweater up and over my head. I raise my arms to help and think I don't know if I want him to do this. I lie back on the bed and my tummy bounces. I can see him looking and I say I don't know why it's so bloated today. He laughs a short laugh and kisses my tummy button and says, You are beautiful. I don't know if he means it but he leans over me and starts kissing more. It's fast and I love his lips but I keep thinking, I keep thinking. He unbuttons the button on my jeans. Pulls. Tugs. Knickers. Socks. Off. And then I'm lying naked on his bed and I feel like a blimp. He kisses my skin and says I taste sweet. He strokes the soft hair on my breasts and tummy and his fingers go further down too. I catch both his hands and hold them fast. I am on my back and he is on my

32

front. He is kissing my cheeks. I speak. Soft. I say, Not today. He stops kissing, looks into my eyes and sees I am looking towards the window. I can see the moon. Peach, he says, his soft breath falls and I turn my face to his. He looks sad. I'm sorry, I say. He closes his mouth, not into a frown, not into a smile. A line that bends a little on the left side of his face. He straightens his arms and turns. He is lying on the bed, on his side, he puts one hand on my stomach and sighs.

I want to talk. To say things to him. Tell him. Talk to him. Say what happened last night when I was walking home. I want to say things but I don't know how to order the words. Sentences slither around my brain. Scattered words. Scatterbrained. Scatter sentences. Scattered semantics. Scattered seeds. Scatter my brains. Grow. Grow, Green. Grow tall. Thick knots on your chest that I touch with my fingers. Thick, not fickle, knots fill you from the inside, out. Brown knots. Not hard. Not wood, or bone. Cartilage, inserted in your holes like cartridges, malignant melanomas, only, no. No cancer. Not cancer, knots can be removed if you please, but please, don't. I like them like that. I place my hands flat. I want to climb the ridges in your skin. But how do I get in? I have put in plugs. Plugged up my hole. Like yours. But so I don't ooze out. Because I will ooze, infect, in fact. I don't want that.

He is looking into my eyes like he's looking for these lines to seep through my skin or slide out of the side of my brain. He kisses me again. His hands move over my bumps, all three. He wants to touch inside me. But he stops. Reverses his hand back over my bulging stomach. Peach? he asks. Are you pregnant? I. Oh. I am struck and slow at thinking. There is something inside. I don't know what it is. His eyes are wide. Wild. Life. Inside. I hadn't thought of that. And then I think about what went inside last night and it was a sausage and what if it got stuck, sticky, somehow there was sperm inside that sausage and I will give birth to a litter of hot dogs? My thoughts spiral. I am silly. I half laugh at the thought of little pink sausages in a cot wrapped in blankets, pigs in blankets, and this time it's a whole laugh. I look up at Green through waterlogged eyes. He looks blurry and offended. And I kiss him saying sorry at the same time. But now to be serious. Maybe Mam is right? Would a baby with Green be so bad because we have been having sex and sometimes some things just happen. Maybe I have been feeling full all day and off food and feeling sick because I am pregnant? I hadn't thought of that. Green impatiently pulls away. Are you pregnant? he asks again and his voice is low and loud and I am sorry for laughing and I say, Maybe. He smiles and pulls me close to his chest, folds me in and I smile and feel strange.

Forest for Rest

I'm having a dream when I open my eyes. The sky is dark brown and spitting soil. Everything that was up is down. Gravity is gone. Cool clouds have caught me. They cover me. I am white. I am wet. My skin is wet. Wait. No. There are clouds below me. I feel the warmth of the sun on my back. But those clouds don't cover me. Not enough. Just thick patches. Bright white and blue in places. Thick white fur. Not fur. I feel. Wet. Moist. Mould. I am moulding. My skin is eating my flesh. Skin sinking. I try to touch the tops of trees with my fingertips, try to reach, try to pull myself out of the clouds. I can't reach. The leaves leave me. Today I decay. I close my eyes to die.

Wet wakes me. I am wet. From sweat. Face down in the damp. Green has grown over me during the night. Light doesn't quite penetrate the hot mist of moss surrounding me. But it's definitely day. I don't remember falling asleep. I turn my head gently to peep at Green. He is sleeping deeply. His breath echoes in his nose and sounds like a snore but softer. His arm is slotted into the small of my back. Gently rising. Gently falling. There is red in his cheeks like little logs are alight in his mouth. But he isn't burning. There is no smoke so there can't be a fire. He's just warm. And he wakes. He peels himself from me. He leaves behind beads of sweat from dream-soaked sleep. He stands over me and smiles. Good morning, beautiful. I slip under the sheets to hide my swelling self. So that's still there. You slept well, I say, watching while he stretches and yawns. His arms touch the ceiling and his jaw touches the floor. Stretching. Tall. His fingers splinter the ceiling and scratch the paint. I watch little white flakes fall. Snow, I say. He twists his neck to see outside, but ends up turning around anyway. He leans on the windowsill, still stretching. Snow, he says. A little. An inch. Or two. He turns and grins. Snow day. No college. And he's right because the telephone ring rings and he runs downstairs to answer it and when he comes back upstairs he says that Spud was on the phone and said that the college was closed for the day. I feel cold now because the wet sweat on my skin has dried so I curl on my side in the sheets and shiver. Good, I say. He bends to kiss me but I stop him. I put my finger to his lips. I outline his mouth with the tip of my finger. Barely touching but I can feel it is smooth like sanded wood. It tickles. His face wrinkles. His eyes shut tight. He smiles. I don't want to be pregnant. His smile stops but doesn't drop. He opens his eyes and I shut mine. I'm scared to see disappointment. I don't want to be a parent, I say quickly. I can't hear the silence it's too concrete to enter my ears. What if he wants? I wish he'd hurry up and say something. His hands are holding my cheeks. I open my eyes and he's looking and it's a good look he's looking good, so good-looking. I smile. Not a straight one. I am a bit surprised. He says in a low voice, I don't want to be a parent either. But if you wanted a baby to keep then I would look after you both. I put my arms around his neck and rest them on his solid shoulders. He puts his face in my hair. I feel relief and warmth. We must check, I say. He says yes. We will go to the chemist. He puts his hand on my stomach. It could be many things, I say. He is nodding. You shower first, he says.

I take a quick shower and then he takes one. I keep some clean clothes here and when he is in the bathroom I put them on. My shirt doesn't button up over my bulge so I try on one of his but that is even tighter and the sleeves reach my knees. I take it off. When he comes back to the bedroom I am standing just in jeans. He's got another big grin for my belly. Peach, what are you doing? I don't know I feel ridiculous. I laugh. My shirt doesn't fit. Your shirt definitely doesn't fit. He growls a laugh. He's rubbing his hair with his towel. Try this. He hands me a black

T-shirt from a drawer which does fit, it stretches. I put my sweater on over it and smile at him. He is dressing and says I look happier today than I did yesterday. He asks how my knuckles are. I blow on them and tell him they're fine. The scabbing grazes got wet in the shower and the skin around them is strange pink when I look. I blow on them again. The scabs are raised and soggy and yellow and sausage-shaped. No, not sausages. Sick of sausages think of something else. Slugs. Infected slugs. The thoughts that come into my head get blown out with the hot air from my mouth. The thoughts are rage and outrageous and out they go. They're not sausages or slugs. They are just scabs. I'll buy some plasters in the chemist to cover them. Peach, he says, pulling my hands down, I'll buy you breakfast.

Kiss on My Lips, Piss on a Stick

My legs feel heavy and I'm dragging my feet. Shovelling snow with my shoes. Leaving lines behind from my lead legs. Green is taking most of my weight in his hand but I feel solid and stiff and heavy. Someone needs some energy, he says, glancing down. I'm okay, I say, staring down into the snow and focusing on my feet. My shoes are made of stone there is treacle in the snow. My feet slump and slide. Careful you don't fall, he says, glancing down again, watching the sleet slip under my feet. It's okay, I'm going slow. And I have plenty of fat to cushion the blow. It's just as well it won't last long, says Green. What do you mean? I say. The weather is changing.

We stop and look up at the sky. Green sees, I don't. My eyes are pulled to the side by bright colour. I watch cars roll in rows in the street on sushi wheels. The tyres are light and don't leave prints but leave little flecks of fish, pink in the snow. The cars move swiftly, a light grip on the ice from the salt in the seaweed. My eyes whirl with the wheels, with the deep green and white and pink and sometimes red and white, rolling on, more white, it's inside out, a California roll, rolling on, roll on California, it's warmer, it's warmer, it's warmer. The white under the wheels is wasting away to water. The road is black and wet and then dry. Green kisses the top of my head. He lets go of my hand and shrugs out of his coat, I hear his shoulders snap. The sun is shining and it's warm and weird. I shield my eyes from the light that bounces off the bonnets and boots of the cars on the road. It's so warm so suddenly. I take off my coat too. Green looks bemused and says, I guess we'll just have to adjust.

So now it's summer when we get inside the chemist. The shop assistants are replacing the cold and flu medicine display with sunscreen, suncream and sunblock stock. I haven't been in here before and I don't know where to go. There are only three aisles but there are eyes in each of them and they may know Mam. And they may tell her they saw me and saw what I was buying and I don't want Mam to know because she gets too excited. This is awkward. Green is already ahead of me. He is bending down to browse the shelves and he turns and gestures and his waving causes a gust of wind, briefly gale force, to fell a shelf full of foaming shower gels. I don't know whether to laugh or cry or hide as a stampede of shop assistants runs to save the shower gels and rearrange them. One takes the time to turn and tut at Green. He looks down and turns red and laughs a little and says sorry. I grab his hand and drag him into the next aisle. I call him a troublemaker and he pinches my bum and I stop feeling awkward and worried because this is almost fine and almost fun and almost like every other day.

We are faced by a row of boxes. In each box there are sticks and sticks and sticks and stickers stuck on the front of the boxes saying in Just 3 Minutes you will know whether you're pregnant or not and how far along you are. The worry comes back a little. How far along would I have to be to become the size of a blimp? How far along is too far along to not be able to abort the blimp, fly through the sky and fall into Hell? That's a dark thought. Don't go there. Back to boxes. Back to sticks. Enough sticks to build a fence but it's a bit late for fences when I'm potentially fertilised and fences are no good when you are completely defenceless. Green has wandered off and is looking at the condoms so I grab the one box that doesn't have pictures of babies on it and go to pay. The shop assistant doesn't pay any particular attention to me or my purchase and I feel relieved. I go outside without Green. So what do I do with this now? Green comes out of the shop and puts his arm around my waist. Where do you want to do this? he asks. I don't know. I guess where our mams can't find out or find it, I say. I don't know what Green's parents would think. I've only met them a few times. They work a lot. My dad would start building a cot before the urine sample had dried. Does the café have a toilet? I ask. Sure, he says, so we go.

The sun is baking my back as we walk. My hand is wet and sticky in Green's and his is just sticky. It feels like my flesh is going to fall from my bones. Soft. And I squish in my shoes as I walk. Summer sucks. We get to the café and I'm soaked. I could stand over a bucket and they could serve me up in a glass with ice. Green grabs a table and I just keep going to the back of the room where the toilets seem to be. Get it over with. There is one unisex toilet in a small cupboard which is more like a cave, concrete and dark. Grey cement walls which the owners haven't got round to painting or were leaving bare to create a prison-cell effect. But I don't know why they would want to create a prison-cell effect, I don't know why anyone would want to create a prison-cell effect and then I realise they probably didn't want to spend any money on paint because this is not the type of toilet to spend time in, the piss is probably still dripping from the penises as they close this door and sit back down to finish coffees. The toilet is silver steel and cold. I sort of sit. Sort of hover. And then I stand. I undo my buttons and open the box and read the instructions, even though I know what to do. I sort of sit, sort of hover and gosh, it still stings. I should probably unstitch the stitches soon. I sit down completely. In three minutes I'll know. I prop the stick on the box and put my head between my legs. I feel the blood rushing to my face. And I stay like that and try to count to a hundred and twenty and lose count at eighty so I just keep my head down until it feels like it's going to drop off. When I sit up my face drains and I feel faint and ignore it. I look at the little window on the stick expecting to see a sausage. I see in big black letters NOT PREGNANT. My heart is in my throat and it is hard to swallow. But mostly I feel flat. I feel hollow. But I'm still fat. I stare at the blank wall and I could be looking in a mirror. I didn't want a baby. I wanted an answer. I guess I got one. I guess I should go and tell Green.

He's got a booth and two menus. I slide on to the bench opposite him and breathe in and breathe in and sit down and breathe out but I can't, I almost burst because my belly is pressed up tight against the table. I'm so red in the cheeks I go blue with embarrassment. Green pulls the table towards him. I can tell he thinks it's funny, the laugh whistles out of his nose but it's not loud. His jaw clicks and snaps his smile. He reaches for my hand and asks me what I want for breakfast and calls me Beautiful. I flick open the menu and flop on it. My face is cooling on the Formica. It was negative, I say. I know, he says. He tickles the back of my neck with the tip of his finger. It's the right result, he says. I know, I nod. I try to smile. I wonder if he's wondering what it is instead, but he's looking at his menu and concentrating and I think he's probably just feeling relief and thinking about food. I don't want to feed this bloating floating boat of a belly. Would you mind if I had meat? he asks. I start to say no as he says, I fancy sausages and I must have gone green because he says he has changed his mind and wants eggs. I'm sorry, I say, have whatever you like, I'm just feeling funny about what happened in the bathroom. I'll just have a glass of water, I say, and he frowns and says, you have to eat.

Once I have convinced him toast and jam will be adequate he gets up to order at the counter. I watch him walking away and I wonder why he hasn't asked more questions or cried or cheered. And he knew already because we are always safe. I don't feel safe now, though. I feel like I could fall off this bench at any moment and roll away. Green turns his head to look and smile at me and I look back at him and do my best 'I'm okay' smile. Still smiling, I turn away and look out the window and put my hand to my mouth and tear the smile from my lips when I see, for just a second, a large, looming sausage pressed against the glass. Shock. I'm in shock. I look around to see if anyone else sees but everyone else in the café is absorbed in eating or drinking, reading a menu, reading a newspaper, wishing they could smoke, something else, anything else. I don't want to look again because I know he is still there. His eyes are boring holes in my flesh and it singes and stings and I look, damn it, I look, I stare back, I stare at him and I want to fucking scream. He is rubbing against the glass just staring with no expression. I can't see his mouth from this angle but I know it is wide, gaping open. He's rubbing and it's squeaking and the squeak is tearing and travelling across the room to me but no one looks up. He's still rubbing, his body is lubricated by the dripping grease against the smooth glass and it's disgusting. I can't look any more and I try to get up, to run to Green, but my bottom is sticking stuck to the spot and my bump just bumps the table. I put my hands over my eyes and try to be somewhere else. And when I am calmer I peep through the parting of my fingers. He is gone but there is a seven-foot grease streak left on the glass and I can't believe no one else saw.

Green brings me back to earth with some soft kisses and then our breakfast comes and my toast is cold. I eat it because Green is watching me and wants me to eat. I can see the grease slipping down the glass out of the corner of my eye. Green grasps my gaze and turns around to look. He says with a frown and mouth full of fried eggs, What is that? I shrug and look down and spread some sticky jam on my brick-bread toast. I take a bite out of a slice. A big bite and I've sliced my tongue with a sharp tooth. I wince and swallow. Taste blood. Taste tongue. Green grabs my hand. A tear streams down my cheek and blood streams down my chin. Green's eyes widen and he leans in. Peach! He wipes my chin with his index finger but gives me a splinter. I laugh and suck my tongue. I pull out the splinter and give it back to him. He laughs. I've got shivers, the tears are still streaming, I'm shaking and scared because I don't know what's going to happen now. I look down at my belly and wonder if Green has a splinter big enough to burst it.

I am quivering, everything is quivering. My fear is so great it makes the whole room shake. The jam in the jam pot jiggles. Cutlery is clattering. The table trembles. Green grins and says Spud really knows how to make an entrance. The quaking continues. Getting greater. It's not my fear. The other people look around at the shaking waitresses and their tottering trays of jarring jam jars and clattering coffee pots but don't look concerned, and carry on.

My belly bounces beneath the table. I grab it to stop it rolling away. Spud. Green prepares for his friend by stretching. He anchors himself by wrapping his legs around mine, he leans back in the bench, brings his long, thin arms to his chest and slowly slowly stretches them out. I hear every branching bone in his body snap. His mouth is gloriously growing into a smile that stretches his arm-span. He says it feels good. I am watching him, smiling and thinking of the muscles that are moving, bending, stretching in his body. In rolls Spud. He doesn't even push the door open, just rolls at it with his weight and with speed, spiralling through the room, tumbling into our table and stopping. The table tilts backwards, forwards. Spud holds the edges of the table with his huge dirty hands. Always dirty. He eases the table to the floor. Everything else that was shaking has stopped, a few things have smashed and everyone else in the café turns to stare at Spud, just long enough to convey their collective annoyance, and then they turn back and carry on.

Spud sticks his stump of an arm out to Green and Green sticks his sticks out. Their hands twist around each other's, both their cheeks turn hot and their smiles grow wide, wild. I look away. I don't have a share in their moment. I feel intrusive. As their arms continue to twist I see only a glimpse of what's gone and grown between, how they grew together. The special moment collapses under the weight of Spud's loud low chuckle. Chortle. All right, Peach? he says. I start to say my reply but it sticks in my throat as my skin rips and I realise what has happened. He might be solid but he is swift. Spud is now sitting next to me and I am squashed between the wall and his solid side. And in the process of putting me here my bottom has become unstuck from the bench and I am pretty sure my skin is stuck to the seat and no longer to me. It stings, slightly. But I am already sore so the sting doesn't stand out for long.

I say, Hi Spud. Green smiles at me. I think he wants us to be friends. And I like Spud, but he and Green have known each other for ever. We'll never be friends like that. And Spud hates Sandy. Peach? Did you hear what we just said? Green is reaching across the table and tickling my chin with his long finger. Huh? I look at Spud, but he's just staring at me like I'm stupid with his wonky eyes. One of his eyes is significantly higher than the other, and kind of in the corner of his forehead. It's not really a corner, though. I don't really notice until I'm up close like this but he's more spherical than square. With a million grooves and bumps and lumps on the surface of his skin. With flecks of dirt everywhere, does the boy never wash? I realise I'm just staring at him and I think I go red because he breaks out into a big chunky smile and I can see his crinkled wet tongue. I laugh. Sorry, Spud, I was miles away. I know, he says, with a chalky chuckle. Do you want to come out tonight? he asks. Oh. No – no thanks, I say, I'm supposed to be looking after Baby tonight for Mam and Dad, I say, quickly. Green looks at me. Are you? he asks. Yeah, I say, I forgot to mention it earlier. Anyway, I'm sure you don't want me tagging along, you guys have fun, I don't mind. Yeah, says Spud, we're only going to the pub. I think he's relieved I'm not coming. Green asks, You don't mind? And I say, Absolutely not, firmly planting my 'go ahead' smile on my lips. Spud says, Excellent, in a low excited rumble. He starts eating my old toast and I push the plate towards him.

Suggestive Jesting

Mam and Dad dive out of the door as soon as I open it. Thanks, babe, Mam says, kissing my cheek roughly. We're going dancing! She puts her hand on her hip, hitches up her knee. She is so happy. She looks so silly, I can't help but smile. Have a great time, I say. Dad says, You're in charge now, Peach. Make sure you lock the door. He pats my head once with his big hand. They wave as they walk swiftly down the street and I can hear Mam saying, Quick, we'll miss the bus. I shut the door. I don't lock it. It's dark in the hallway but I can see light under the living-room door. I should lock it. So I do.

I don't know what to do with myself. After silently dancing around the house in my pyjamas for a really long time and dancing silently beside Baby asleep in his cot and feeling silly, I go into the living room and decide to watch TV. I think I should study but I'm too distracted. A bit happy and unfocused. Loose and juicy. I laugh. I switch the lights on in the living room, the low lamps that glow. I go straight to the sofa, but glance at the mantel. I see letters. A lot of letters. I pick up the pile and settle on the sofa with one leg curled under myself. I count the letters. Seven. All for me. All in the same kind of envelope. All slightly stained, all scrawled in the same scrawling gnarly loathsome lettering. All. All with the same grease. All with that same sickening scent. One envelope has a Post-it note stuck on the front. From Dad. *These came for you, Peach, more love letters. Love Dad*, it said. I want to slap him. No I don't. I used to wait. I remember. I think about my penfriend. What was her name? Tiny. I used to wait. I used to write to Tiny once a week. No. Once a month. And I would sign the letter and lick the envelope with love. I was eleven. And I would send the letter. And I would wait for a reply immediately. Sit by the letter box and wait for a reply. I forget who stopped writing first. I'm thinking of all this, staring at the letters in my hands through eyes that can't see. They're bleared up. Full up with tears. I'm hot and full up with fucking frustration. Rage. My arms are shaking. Hatred coats my tongue. Fuzz on bad fruit. I rip open the first envelope. My eyes are flooded and don't see the obscenity. I rip the next, the next, the next, the next, the next, the last. And before I know, I'm sat in snow. Paper flakes flutter. As they fall into my hot rage I hear them singe and sizzle.

Decisive Incising

Snip. Don't slip. Snip. Don't slip. Snip. Snip. Slip and I will shear and that's the fear the fear the fear. I thought doing this in the mirror was a good idea but I can't coordinate my movements. I look at my reflection. My arm is violently trembling. I put the scissors down on the towel in front of me. I push myself up with my knuckles pressed on the rug, try to make my back fit flatly against the bathroom wall. It's cold. I take my shirt off. My skin blisters immediately with goose-bumps and every tiny hair pricks up and I look in the mirror and laugh because I look like a cactus. A cactus with legs. A cactus that planted itself on top of something with legs. Something with legs wide apart and a vagina that's been split but is hopefully now healed and I'm not laughing any more. The cold is distracting. A natural numbing agent. I don't know why I thought I could remove stitches with the kitchen scissors.

Getting up takes too much time. I crawl out of the bathroom and head for the stairs. I try to crawl slowly but my belly bounces forward and I am led by my lead dead weight. The carpet scrapes my knees and then they feel cool when I crawl on the cold kitchen tiles. I don't know why the sewing box is kept in the kitchen. I take out the small scissors from the box. I've got an urge to put them in my mouth. I clutch them in my hand and crawl back to the bathroom. I don't even try to stand, I think I would fall right back down again.

I resume my position. Legs apart. Back against the wall. My hand is still shaking. And I just think. Be quick, be quick, be quick. I snip. I snip through each stitch. That is not the hard part. I reach for a towel and stuff as much as I can fit in my mouth. Bite down hard. I'm not scared of the pain. I am so accustomed to the constant sting. But the thought of unthreading these stitches makes my teeth retract into my skull and my toes curl backwards. I feel dizzy. I feel sick. I feel. I put down the scissors. I shut my eyes. I inhale through my nostrils deeply. I feel for the thread. And. Pull.

I don't remember how many stitches I put in to begin with, and I don't count how many times I pull on threads, but when I open my eyes and look in the mirror, I can see that all the stitches are out. And on the floor in front of me are a few little black curls, threads that look like eyelashes. I spit the towel out and exhale. I wipe my mouth with my forearm. I can't believe it. There's no blood. There's no seeping fluid. There are small pink pinpricks. I'm so happy. I start laughing. I stop laughing and listen. Is Baby crying? I think my laughter shook the shocked silent bathroom.

I feel shocked too, but not silent any more. I think I've been in shock since it happened. I think this is the start of the end of this terrible time. I gulp. I say to myself, Let's pretend that this never happened. I don't want to be a victim. One of those victims. Oh this awful thing happened to me when I was young. He stole a piece of me (said in a raspy, broken voice) … a piece of my soul. I cringe and crinkle at the cliché. I'm a strong, solid person. I look at myself in the mirror, at my bulging stomach. Evidently a solid person. I grin a little. And it's far more like he gave me a piece of him, than taking a piece of me. I cringe, again. Poke at my belly button. Go down! I say out loud. Shrink, won't you? I listen again. Baby is still sleeping. I should check on him. I don't hear Sid padding around. I wonder where he is. I get up off the floor. With some effort.

I want to wake Baby and do a dance with him around the house. Play music. Loud. Laugh. Feel his weird wiggling warm cheek against mine as we chuckle for no reason, feel my knees buckle, for no reason other than sheer joy. I float through the house to Baby's room, to Baby's cot. I look at him sighing in his sleep, his mouth making a tiny o. I press the soft sheet around his squidgy body. He doesn't stir. I smile at his peace and think a simple blessing. He feels it fall upon him and smiles without waking.

I go back to the bathroom. I want to shower and show outwardly how fresh I feel inside. I need to do something with my hair! I exclaim aloud to myself in the mirror, raising my hands to the hopeless bush on my head, and frown so hard I go cross-eyed and when I refocus my gaze, my furry, exasperated twin appears and then disappears and we both sort of laugh.

I'm already naked so I don't undress. I put the shower on, make the water hot, turn the knob to POWER: HIGH. I step into the bath, under the water, and pull the curtain round. OW. Wow. My head fills with hot steam and my skin with hot drop-let pins. I wonder if this is what actual acupuncture feels like. Eyes shut tight. I whip my hair up into an ice-cream swirl of shampoo. Through the foam and steam and stream of water swirling down the drain and the sound of water spearing skin and ceramic I can hear the phone ring.

Waiting Room

Green's got no recollection. He had his collection knocked out of him. How will he recollect it? But Spud remembers. It's hard to tell whether it's dried blood or mud on Spud. Dried blood makes him a hero. He's reeling, rolling, rocking. He doesn't flinch with my hand on his shoulder, I think he even softens. He is still a heaving, shuddering, mud-clad mass. I tried, he says. I say, I know, and I'm grateful. It's not your fault.

He jumped us out of nowhere! Spud exclaims. He scratches his bald head, leaving dark marks on his waxy skin. He doesn't look at me when he speaks. I don't think he can see with a fat black swollen closing eye. But he reaches for my fingers and touches me with his gritty palm. He lets go when I bend down and kneel in front of him on the hospital linoleum. Bending and kneeling takes time, adds ceremony, and I pluck my gasp of pain out of the air which is left hanging, put it back in my mouth and swallow it on my way down. I hope he hasn't heard it, but then he may have mistaken it for one of his own, as we put our hands to our mouths simultaneously. A rare, stray tear has escaped from the eye that is not closing and is making its way down his angular cheek, pushing mud and/or blood out of the way. His face is yellow and grey and bruised and all glowing under the strip lighting above us. And his tear falls on my jeans.

The thing is … this thing is … Peach … he said your name. This thing … this huge guy … He was like … this violent fucking machine. He didn't say anything else. Just your name. And then he just started pounding him. Over and over. In the face. Everywhere. Green didn't even stand a chance. And Green is hard, Peach. But this guy … His mission was to make minced meat. But Peach, it's like he knew you. He says this, looking into my face. He's looking for something. My recollection.

I look at Spud and then quickly down at the floor. His eyes (well, the good one) are like shoots, growing with every patient blink. Spud, I don't know, I say, steadily. I'm staring at the blue floor until it fuzzes, my vision fades with the flow of tears. Do you want to see him? I say, still looking down. I can see Spud's shadow, shaking his head. I think it's bad, Peach, I'm not good with stuff like this. I hate hospitals. I got to go. I say I understand. I touch the top of his head. To my surprise his skin is smooth. He lets me for a second and then starts to shudder. I say I will call him if anything changes. He says he will come again tomorrow. I thank him. Thanks, Spud, I say. If you weren't there ... He stops my sentence. I should've done more, I could've killed this guy, this ... thing. Made him into fucking mash. His rage rattles his entire solid structure. A cage. Caged in. He caves in. He crumples. I'll see you tomorrow, he says in a sad slow whisper, and rolls away.

Hospitality

Bloodletting. Let in blood. I'd give you mine but I've lost a lot too. I think back to Mr Custard's class on blood components, I try to remember how long the human body takes to regenerate blood cells. I shut my eyes and see black and red and white spots and soon I'm zooming off on a red spot, a red cell, an erythrocyte, sailing, surfing on a red sea. Circling the pool. Skimming the shore, reaching with my arms stretched wide, touching the sides. Transparent. Apparently a plastic bag. Thick plastic. I steady myself on the cell, not losing speed. I suck my last breath in. Shut my eyes and. Sink. Into the thick. Viscous. Smooth. Like paint, like oil. Smells like metal in the rain. I sink, I slip through. Feet first and belly tucked to be thin. Through the tube, for inches, for minutes. Slip and drip. And drip. And drip. Through the skinny plastic straw penetrating your skin. Into your vein. I see my red-cell friend through to the end. Touch him with thanks for his help and his hope and say I hope to see you soon in the glow of Green's cheeks and then he will have a kiss.

When I get back from my transfusion trip, Green's eyes are open and his voice is lower than a grave and sounds like crunching gravel.

I hold both his hands. Sitting in the chair by his bed, I have to shift and shove my bulge out of the way to reach him. His arms are bandaged and he can't stretch. My stomach is solid and sore but I don't care. I bury my head deep in his blankets, try to burrow into him. He is softer than usual. Like a sapling, or a pile of wet leaves and soft sticks. He holds my hand but his grip has gone and I feel like I am holding and he is held. I don't want to cry now. I want him to see me strong. I bring my head close to his. Peach, he says, slow and slurred. I'm here, I say. Try not to talk. I reach to touch his grey cheek.

We stay silent and soft. Green falls back into a deep sleep. I am glad at this and loosen up a little. I relax my shoulders and bend slowly to place my face in his lap, but as I tilt my head I am startled to see someone slip into the room. Someone. Something. The room is lit by a single lamp, a single slip of light on Green's face. The rest of the room is covered with sheets of shadow. I can't see. I squint into the dark. My thoughts rush to the alley in the dark and his sickening slick shadow. I don't want to think about him. I grip Green's hands hard and then let go. Rage runs razors through my veins, rips them open, rips me open, shows red, screams red, I drip red rage on to crisp white sheets. How could he slip in here unnoticed? But then I remember his stealth. His sly sneaking, his sickening power. And I don't have a weapon. I don't have defence. I search the darkness for a needle, syringe, something. Nothing. All I have is fear, rage, dread and a half-dead boyfriend.

I am vibrating with tension and tiredness. I remain still, silent and staring. And then I see.

Silver silent spectres sail. Silent as they dance, slow and shy. Faces facing down to the floor. Moving in soft waves, silent, soft flourishes. Silvery silhouettes silhouetted by the glowing green lights of gory medical machinery. Glimmering, shivering like silver fishes in oily streams. Shy and silent, but subtly surveying. Seeing everything. Softly sashaying around the room. Seeing me sit, sigh, cry. Silently soothing me with their soft presence. I see now in the glowering light their slight movements, slipping new sheets on the bed, sliding off old bandages, winding new ones around wet wounds, twisting new fluid bags on to long plastic lifelines. All in swift silent motion. I strain my eyes to see clearly but they dance away into the darkness and I realise that I am half dumb half numb have been asleep and awake and two days have passed I have not stood or walked or talked until the doctor comes in and then I am automatic, nodding, smiling, picking up the phone and dialling Dad. Green is discharged.

Recovery

You need to sleep, I say. I pull the covers back and help Green to sit down on the bed. I'm fine, Peach, I promise. I hear the poorly hidden strain in his voice. You need to rest tonight, I say. And when your parents come back tomorrow, we're going to talk to the police and we're going to— I am silenced by Green's cold finger touching my lips. Stay with me tonight, he says. I can't, I say, pulling his heavy shoes off, pushing his log legs up on to the bed. I gently push his shoulder, to try to get him to lie down. He doesn't resist and I am relieved. I can't battle. I pull the covers up to his chin. He looks like a plank, a pile of building materials covered in a dustsheet, awkward, waiting, ready to be put to work. I stand and stroke his forehead. He is chuckling beneath my touch, I feel the sheet quivering. What's so funny? I say and as I look down I realise that my belly is resting on his face, and he can't breathe properly. I grasp my gut. I am embarrassed. I turn away and he places a hand on my back. I'm sorry, Peach, I didn't mean to upset you. I'm not upset, I say. I am upset. I am mortified. It just keeps growing and bulging, ballooning. Perhaps it's time to see a doctor, he says softly. I turn back to him and kneel down slowly by his side. I realise when I'm on the floor that I won't be able to get back up again without help. I rest my head on the side of the bed and curse quietly. He runs his twiggy fingers through my hair. Not until you're well, I say. I have enough to worry about. His fingers stop moving, his hand becomes heavy on my head. His deep breathing whips up a light wind that gently brushes my hair against my face and swings the open door lightly. I stay on the ground by his bed all night, bobbing slightly in the breeze of his breathing. I am a beached whale, a bobbing marooned buoy. I'm tired but I don't sleep. I am scared. I wonder if I am watched. The stench of Lincoln lingers on Green's skin. I stay awake and watch for shadows.

Wail (Whale) in the Water.
Besides, the Sea

I try to keep my feet dry but I can't see where I'm walking. The bathing suit is stretched tightly over my tummy, the black exhausted Lycra groans as I pull the straps up higher to try and release the constriction around my middle. It doesn't work and I get a slap on the shoulders as the straps snap back. I pad across the grey stone tiles. My footsteps thud and thump and slap and splash through little puddles of dirty cold water. My toes grip the tiles to stop me from slipping. Sullen speech and subdued splashes echo off locker-lined walls. I look up to the high ceiling and follow the strip lights to the poolside. SHOWER FIRST, PEACH! shouts Trunk from her deckchair tower. I nod and step into the shallow basin which is filled with filthy grey stagnant water. I wade through it to hit the tap on the wall. Water slaps my ankles, splashes up my legs, clings to my skin, a biofilm is formed, bacteria bites, I'd better shower quick before the infection sets and my legs get eaten and there is nothing to support my boulder belly. I turn in a circle under the cold chemical shower. My skin sizzles. I shut my eyes so they don't burn. The smell of chlorine is strong. I inhale deeply and feel a little buzz in my brain. I turn slowly, savouring the tingle on my skin and the warmth it brings to my body. Chemical. Corrosive. For a short, sweet moment I am a glorious black globe spinning in space before the sun. If I stand under the shower long enough my skin might burn off. Burn off the broken flesh the damage the dirt the hurt. Might see what is underneath, what is growing inside. I open my eyes and catch Trunk's stare as I turn around. Her black beady eyes shine in the neon-yellow light. She is glaring at my gut and I pretend I don't see her. I put my hands to my tummy and step out when the water stops spluttering out of the shower head. I hold my belly firmly so Trunk can't see me wobble. She shouts at me across the pool: WHERE'VE YOU BEEN, PEACH? I MISSED YOU YESTERDAY. AND YOU LOOK FAT NOW.

I look at my reflection in the pool as it waddles on the waves. She's right. My face is bright red, flushed with shame and sore from the caustic cleanse. I am fat now. I don't know how. I'd better start swimming. And I jump I dive, try to dive, belly flap, belly flop slop slosh into the pool.

The water is cool and soothing. I can hear Trunk shouting about the tidal wave I sent to her from the pool, across the tiles toppling her tower of chairs. I don't care. I swim to the surface slowly. I am sluggish, I am slow. The weight of my stomach pulls me under but I resist. I twist my arms into a flailing front crawl. Thrash splash and crash. I throw water forward fast. Force. But I'm not moving forward. I try to shuffle, shoulder my way to the side of the pool, hold on and float. There are other swimmers in the pool. Some of them are really into it, blowing up bubbles to the surface and sailing low slow in the water. Hair Netty is here. She is sweeping the surface of the pool with a gorgeous gracious backstroke. Her body is dark brown where fat has spat at her from stoves for years, weathered leathery like a shoe. Her long dark hair fans out behind her, leaving little droplets of oil on the water as she glides, tiny shiny pearls, pretty. Watching her I am calm and soothed. She turns smoothly in the water and begins a length of breaststroke. The skin on her back is white and rubbery. She's like an uncooked sausage that has been burnt on one side. I can't look at her once that thought is formed. She swims by me underwater and sends up little bubbles that squeak when they pop on the surface. I return her greeting with a wave under the waves.

I turn and swim slowly to find my balance in a soft breaststroke. I feel the oil in the water left behind by

Hair Netty and watch the traces of rainbows it leaves on the surface. The water is smooth. I feel soothed. I follow the little pearlescent orbs of oil that sail my way and begin to relax into my swim. I glance up at Trunk as I go by, she is shouting at someone peeing in the kiddie pool. I swim the length of the pool once, turn and follow the oil-patch path, take a big breath, push down and swim under the water. My breath is short, my belly is buoyant, pushes up, crushes my lungs. I can't hold my breath as long as I could and I am surprised, splutter and splutter and suck in water, gulp in greasy water so greasy, tastes so meaty. Terrifying. Tangy on my tongue, the memory comes flooding back, flowing, flooding flood in my lungs, stopped up, tight fright water-tight. Coming up. Cough. For. Cough up for. Cough. Air. Cough up. Cough cough. Coughing. Catch more water that sticks in my throat, greasy thick globules in my gullet, hard to swallow, easy to choke. He's here. This is not the gentle grease of continual cooking. This choking thick suffocating swallowed slime is the excrement of evil. Sludge in my lungs drags me down. I don't want to drown. I throw my arms up and splash, thrash, try to keep my head up, try not to look down into the water where the dark sinister shadow of Lincoln lurks. I thrash, I crash into the side of the pool, colliding with the tiles. Trunk grips my hand, grabs my arm and drags me up. My stomach scrapes against the side of the pool, scoring my bathing suit, grazing my gut. I'm rolled on to the cold surface of the poolside. Trunk slaps my back and I spew gunky muck water. She drags her hand across my mouth and pushes me firmly on my back. Kneeling over me she shrieks, PEACH! PEACH! SPEAK TO ME! SPEAK! CAN YOU HEAR ME! Before I can answer she brings her lips to mine and kisses. Kisses. Trunk! Stop! I say through stuck sucked lips. I'm fine I'M FINE! I can't move from under her solid wide weighty cylindrical shape. I manage to free my arm and poke my finger into her dense body. She unpuckers, stops sucking and pulls away immediately. PEACH, I SAVED YOU WITH THE KISS OF LIFE, she bellows. She stands and helps me up. YOU'RE SO FAT YOU WERE DROWNING. She puts her arm heavily around me and lifts me to the shower. She puts me under and hits the tap. THERE YOU ARE, PEACH, NO NEED TO THANK ME. I SAVED YOU. DON'T TRY TO SWIM UNTIL YOU ARE THIN AGAIN. Her pinprick eyes push out of her chunky face to latch on to my belly and bore into it. She turns and trundles back to her deckchair tower but her eyes still stick out, still beam at me from the back of her head. I shudder and slump against the cold stone wall.

Shivering, my legs quiver, I move slowly towards the lockers. He's here. He's found me. Here. He's following me. I flip my head around quick, expecting him to have slithered up silently behind me. My skin crawls away from my skeleton at the thought. He's not behind me, not there. I hold on to the metal as I walk towards the lockers. My fingers move across the cold steel surface, slip over the surface, slipping slippery, I pull my fingers away and look at them, shiny residue stinking of fat and flesh. I look at the locker. The one I have used. It looks like all the other lockers. Exactly the same. But he knew. He has been here. He has pressed his foul body against the locker. Rubbed and rolled and left a filthy film of gruesome grease dripping down the locker door. I grit my teeth as I unlock the door. A folded piece of paper lies on top of my folded clothes. Perfectly placed. I pull my towel out from underneath my clothes. I always forget to put it on top. The nasty smell of raw sausages wafts from the stained page as it flutters in the air, misplaced by the movement of the towel, and it slips to the floor, falls open, face up in a dirty puddle. It instantly absorbs the water and sticks to the tiles. I don't need to bend to read the words. Large letters all cut from tabloid papers. The water runs the ink as I read the letters bleed, the words seep. *I've seen you naked don't run I want your f u z z I lov e Y O u.*

The chemicals in the water have separated the stuck-down letters from the page and they float away. I throw the towel around my shoulders, grab my clothes and lock myself in the nearest changing cubicle. I dry myself quickly, barely dry, my skin will chap and chafe. I struggle into my clothes. Run out. Run home. Run to Green. I don't know where to go and I'm not really running. This weight, this what? What is this? I thump my stomach hard as I waddle away. No speed. Nothing will stop him. I'm so so scared.

I Found You in the Dim Light of Sorrow

I haven't seen him for days, I say. Don't worry, says Dad. He'll come back when he's hungry. He swings Baby over his shoulder and runs swiftly up the stairs. I can hear Mam giggling from the bedroom and the door clicking shut. In unison they shout loudly: GOODNIGHT, PEACH. I close the door on the shrill sounds of sex that ensue.

I lie down on the sofa and shut my eyes. My hands fall straight down to touch my tummy. Strange. How strange it is. Naturally grasping the firm mass doesn't feel so strange any more. The lump I have been lugging though loathsome heavy hurting full, it feels like me, like part of me. Ingrained. Embedded. I think about cells, multiplying, millions, every second, every millisecond for millions of seconds how big can I get? How big will I be before I burst? Cells linking, holding hands, making chains, chains winding, chains winding around my core. Spores sporing, pouring. I wonder what is inside. I wonder what it looks like. I wonder what a doctor will do. Slice me open, pop me with a pin, let me wither, shrivel, dry up, die. I roll off the sofa, over to the window. I stare out into the black night. There must be blackness inside me, dark and hard. My form is lit warmly and reflected in the window. I press my face up close against the cold glass to see deep in the dark. I am worried about Sid. He's not on the wall, or on the lawn where he sleeps under the bush. I look out past the garden to the street. It's difficult to see, it's so dark. I see the street lamp, glowing dimly, orange and dirty. Where I once saw Lincoln sickly swinging. I see his sadistic shadow now. I will always see it. Ingrained. In my brain when I shut my eyes. With my head still pressed against the glass I shut my eyes. The street light glows, penetrates the thin skin of my lids. The light is orange and red and flickering, licking and flicking my eyes, fast like flames. I wonder if the flickering is because it has just started raining. The rain thud thudders against the window, the glass shudders as the rain falls hard. I open my eyes to see water streaking and streaming down the window, distorting the darkness.

And in the darkness I see why the light is flashing. Familiar fear floods me. I'm hot and sticky, dripping sweat suddenly. He's here again. He's there outside. I squint hard to see through the streaked windowpane. Swinging. Swinging. But the swing is swifter. And the shape is smaller. There is no menacing rhythm, no leering. Just a swift shift between light and dark, a small shape beaten by the rain, blowing in the wind. The fear rushes away. Heart stops pumping. Heart stops. Veins drain. Gut-wrenched, I spit from the pit of my stomach, rising up guttural and raw, a mournful moan, ragged and broken. Ragged and broken. When my heart restarts, blood does not flow. I am filled I am saturated with hate. I throw open the front door. My steps are slow but steady. I walk through the deluge. Where are my shoes? I'm not wearing any shoes. Water rushes around my feet and seeps into my socks, soaked. The walk is short but takes time. Took time. Time has been taken and has ended. Time has stopped. The rain has stopped. The wind has stopped the world has stopped. Nothing moves but I am spinning. I can't focus my vision, I can't see. I brush my wet dripping hair out of my eyes and bring my head up slowly to look. The light shines brightly into my eyes, brighter now, sharper, shining grotesquely to display the horror. He hangs. He has been hanged. He hangs from a thin short rope. My howl hurtles through the stillness of the street. I slam to my knees, the concrete cracks under my weight. Kneecaps crack. I wail. Peach! PEACH! Someone is calling my name. The sound reaches me when the hand does, the hand that grabs my shoulder and helps me to my feet and sits me on the wall. I watch through bleary eyes as Dad runs back into the house and brings the ladder and the scissors and climbs the ladder and cuts the rope and cradles the small broken body. He runs with it into the house and comes back for me. He tries to lift me over his shoulder but I am too heavy. I can't move to help him. He puts his arm around me and drags me into the house, sits me on the sofa and wraps a towel around me. He has wrapped him in a towel too and is cradling him by the fire in front of me. Then I realise Dad is only wearing his pants.

What's going on, why are you shrieking, Peach? You'll wake Baby. Mam tuts, sucks her lips together. Then she sees. Dad, cradling Sid. He's dead.

You've Seen the Butcher

I wait in the dark. Pitch dark. I squeeze into a doorway, negotiate my belly into the narrow gap between two red-brick walls. The bricks push me, put pressure on each side of my stomach. If I squeeze in any more I might burst, pop, split and squirt my building boiling venom all over the rain-slicked street. I could burst with hurt. With hate. And show my core. I wait.

I look ahead at the glowing orange street light. I still see the swinging outline of Sid, strangled, strung up, soaked in his own blood and staring with hollow eye sockets, home to fat slithering maggots. I swallow the sick that creeps up my oesophagus, swallow it back into my grimy gut. I warm it there, let it churn let it turn and turn to fuel my ferocity.

I feel the damp wood behind my back, fine droplets of fluid soak into my sweatshirt. Could be rain, could be piss. It stinks. But I let it sink into me. I am dirty. I am driven. I clutch the knife close to my chest. I want to tuck it up under my clothes to feel close to the steel, to touch it to my skin, to rake the blade over the fuzz of my flesh, feel the sharp edge, I could slip it in and sit it deep inside my bones. The sharp edge. The edge. The edge I am on, I am on edge, standing on a ledge with the drop to oblivion below me.

I grip the knife handle tight in my hand. My palms are dry. This is right. I wait for him and watch for his shadow in the glowing orange light.

Knife Party

I smell him before I see him. The stench of rotting pig meat overwhelms the stagnant damp air of the alleyway. The air is dense with grease globules. I see his swollen form slither along the pavement. He is solid and bulging, erect and rolling towards me. I see the slits in his face open wide when he sees me, black slits opening wide, inside is blackened pink pig gristle bristling.

I stand still. Solid. Rigid. Waiting. He slithers towards me. He slides along until he is directly opposite me, pulls himself up, standing, in front of me, two feet taller. My eyes meet his chest, where his sternum should be, but instead thick chunks of gristle and flesh pushing tightly against wafer-thin shiny translucent skin.

His enormous engorged form fills the doorway. He blocks out the light. His thickness touches my tummy, I hold myself in, the hardness pushes against my spine. It is fine. This won't take long.

Mouth open, he spews his lust all over me. I breathe it in and take it deep into my lungs. Fuel for my fight. Fuel my fight. Fuel my hate. Burn. Fuck. Fight. Knife. Fight. Knife. Find. Find the hateful face. The knife moves fast, flashing silver chrome, slips into the slit of his mouth and rips it down. He falls back in shock. He rocks, rolls, falls to the concrete. I dislodge myself from the doorway and fly. I straddle his shuddering slippery body. He is wet, wiggling, wet, wriggling, slippery like a fish but my weight is firm and holds him face down to the ground. The knife drives into his puckered flesh. Punctures. Pricks. The blade penetrates deep. He writhes. He squeals. He screams. I love you, he screams. I love you, he screams. I weep. I stab. I weep. I stab. Lie there, Lincoln. Let the blade lick you, slick, slice slip stuck in your fat. And fissure. My thighs slip and slide over his mottled skin, lubricated by the grease that seeps from the slashes. Grease splashes. He spasms beneath me, contorting, his casing crinkles. His final cry flits and splits through the flurry of violence. I drop the knife. It clangs on the concrete. I stand and stare at his quickly wrinkling form. I am calm.

Plastic Present

Moon has joined lamplight. Orange, white, silver, gold, shining. A glimmering sheen on the obscene scene. Gloaming. Shimmering slithers, incandescent sinew. Life lingers in the withering skin. I watch until the shrivelling is complete. Death winds around the wounds, ascending from the stuck marks, deep cuts.

On my knees I survey the destruction. Limp lifeless loathsome. Love. Love, he said. Love he said. Love. I lack. I lack. No comprehension. My body goes slack. I lie down next to him. Wet street. Grease seeps. I roll on my side and smell his skin. It is thin. So thin. Bluish tinge. See-through. I see through. Lumps of white lipid. Meat minced. Cartilage. Crust. Bits. Collected together. Corrupt. Gnarled gristle. I touch with timid fingers. Smooth. I run my finger round the curve of his girth, it slips easily, lubricated by the oozing juices. I press the slippery case and feel the bumps bobbles nobbles beneath. Feels cold, not cold from being dead but cold like fresh from the fridge. It is not what I remember from that night. Cool, smooth, unmoving. I smell. My nose is close. The reek of raw meat is overwhelming. Wet rancid. Insidious.

I roll away from the flaccid greying flesh. Greying as clouds cover the moon. From my pocket I pull out the roll of black refuse sacks and begin unrolling. I pull them apart, the perforated lines pop. My fingers slip on the plastic, oiled, slick, no need to lick, the plastic parts, I pull open the bag and put it beside me. The dismemberment plan. Hack and stack. Chop. Stop. Neat slices. Slowly. The knife is good. It splits the case with little force and cuts through the clots of fat and flesh. I stack the rounds into the bags with speed. The smell is unreal. I push air out through my nose and swallow but it still seeps in. Toxic. I tie each bag with a tight knot. I bundle the black bags together. He fills six. I hoist four, throw them over my shoulder. I drag two.

I drag. My body sags under the weight. Dead weight. Weighing me down. My heart my head my arms my legs are dragging, being dragged I stagger. I sob. I am crying heavy tears, shuddering. I shake I break with frustration. I am held under dragged under I am underwhelmed.

I drag. Sweat meets the grease on my brow, can't penetrate it, can't cleanse or cool, slides over it, runs into my eyes, mingles with the tears I am crying. I thought I would feel. I thought I would feel better.

I thought I would feel lighter. Less weight. Not this death, not this dead weight. Legs of lead, head hung. This solid crass mass stuck in my stomach should lift, should leave. But it festers, it offends. A taut tumour. Please don't spread. Still the dread lingers. Still dread. I thought the death would expel. Shadows stay, playing in my mind. I put down the bags to wipe my eyes. I rub the grease from my brow with the back of my hand and smell it. The stench stinks, I breathe it in. Rage still, rage, rage I could feed. I will feed. I will eat the fear, the loathsome offender. I will feed. Not breed, not brood. I will eat the food of fear. I will shit later and feel better.

Chop Chop

What's all this, Peach? Mam is eyeing the stacks of sacks I pile on the kitchen floor. She is making cups of tea. Where have you been? Why do you look so dirty? You need to have a shower. She pulls one of the sacks up on to the kitchen table and tears the black plastic open. She sticks her head in the bag. Wow! Where did you get all this, Peach? Get a whiff of that! She draws breath deeply. Her eyes emerge from the dark sack, the pit of raw flesh, boggled and wide, blind with lust. This is the good stuff. Her mouth is open and she licks her lips. I put my hand to my mouth. I can't look at her. I put my head down on the table. I am exhausted. I am filthy. I am filth. Oh yeah this is great. She pulls a large knife from the block and a roll of cling film from the drawer. So fresh. What a find! Dad! Come in here and look at this. Just look at it! Dad bursts through the kitchen door with Baby slung over his shoulder. He swings around. Sugar sprinkles from Baby's bottom, showering the room in a sweet white layer. The falling sugar on the nasty plastic bags sounds like Sandy shifting in his seat. A pure sprinkling of white won't hide the hacked mangled mess of flesh. Won't hide my detest. Give me the sweet white light. I take him from Dad and hold him tight. I lick his little cheek for comfort and he chuckles and wiggles in my arms. He sniffs at my skin, snuffles and sneezes. I don't want him to be contaminated by the filth. I hold him further away from me but I don't want to let him go. His sweetness saves me.

Dad has one hand on Mam's bottom and one arm elbow deep in a sack. His lips are wet, little droplets of spittle have formed at the corners of his mouth. This is great, Peach. All this meat – you don't even eat it! Brilliant! Let's have a barbecue tomorrow. It tastes best fresh! He smacks Mam's bottom playfully. She giggles gleefully. Yes! A barbecue, says Mam. She is unrolling the roll of cling film on the table, spreads it out and smooths it. She takes a chunk of flesh from the bag and squeezes it in her hand. Her tongue stays out of her mouth as she concentrates. She lays the meat out in little lumps. Little lumps of Lincoln. Little lifeless lumps. She wraps the flesh tightly in cling film, film clings, a shiny skin, meat pushing against the membrane, engorged. She twists the ends of the plastic wrap and holds it up proudly. Looks like sausages, says Dad. These will cook up nicely!

Baby is mesmerised by Mam's meat processing. Meat procession. They roll in a row along the table, taut-tied and terrifying. She works fast with the fatty flesh, rolling the glistening gristle. She has grease on her forehead from brushing her hair back from her face. I watch her. What a feast, what a feast, she murmurs as she rolls out her little sausage soldiers. Reconstructing the horror. Multiplying the monster. I murdered. Murdered the monster that stalked, shocked with violence. Loathsome life. I took. Took life. Life ended. Ended. Eliminated. Evil, evil. Eradicated. And here is Mam reanimating the wretched man with such vigour. I want to laugh. I should cry. The horror, the horror. It's over. Is it over? Baby has gripped a sausage in his fat hand and is squeezing it tightly. I take it from him and he starts to cry. Let him play, Peach, says Dad. I put him on my shoulder to soothe him but he wails and wails, wants to hold a sausage and wriggles towards the table. Set him down here, Peach, says Dad, piling the sausages high. The tabletop shimmers, slick with slime. I can't contaminate Baby, sit him down in that poison. But what harm now? Just soiled, just spoiled sausage meat. Dad stops shovelling the slabs of flesh and stares at me until I sit Baby down on the table. Go and shower, Peach. I'll make you a cup of tea, he says.

Subdued

After the shower I sit soaking wet with my towel wrapped around me. Shivering. I feel weak. I am spent. Shock. Rage. Horror. Grief. Guts. Revenge! All spent. All simmering down. Thick adrenaline, thinning. Dissipating. Leave me. Leaving me weary. I am so thirsty. I go into the bathroom and run the cold water tap. Stick my head under the faucet and lap lap lap. The water is fresh and rolls down my throat so fast. Feels clean. And what now? What do I feel? What have I done?

I get into bed and roll between the cold sheets. My skin prickles. My bump my lump makes the turns difficult. Is it softer? Is it hollow? Will it shrink quickly? I want to call Green to tell him it's okay now. To tell him it will all be okay.

I feel relief.

Before sleep creeps up on me and presses my eyelids down with soft warm fingertips I stare into the dark and think about the shapes and shadows he made to destroy and I am not scared now and I don't regret.

Boom. Blast! At Last

I comb my hair carefully, smooth and separate the tangled strands. I curl my eyelashes. Pinch my cheeks. Put on make-up. Make up my face to smile and show that I am well and all right and will be all right. I pat down my shirt. My belly bursts between the buttons. I have nothing else to wear. I don't suppose anyone will be looking at me. I don't suppose I look that bad. I grin at the mirror, my teeth are clean, my lipstick looks ridiculous. Mam will be pleased. Music and voices drift through the open window on a sweet spring breeze.

Green's grin is wide and smiles the width of the mirror. He stands in the doorway with his head bent forward. You look lovely, Peach. I make a face at him in the mirror and spin around smiling. I go to him and hug him hard but my belly is in the way, I can't get close enough to rest my head on his chest. He lifts my chin up to kiss. His mouth is mossy-soft and moist. I gently touch the black bruise on his cheek.

Black in this light, blue in that. It's healing, he says in a whistling whisper. His spindly fingers reach around my back, my body and rest on the top of my bump. I'm going to see a doctor tomorrow, I say. Good, says Green. I'm sure they'll be able to help. I hope so, I say. Trunk nearly fell off her tower when she saw me! Take no notice, he says; she just wants you for her team, he says, chuckling. Everyone is here, Peach. Do you smell that? Smoke and the smell of charred flesh floats through the window. Dad is cooking up a storm out there. What will you eat, Peach? My smile is wide when I say I'm trying something new today. My laugh is loose and unlike me lately. Green smiles and kisses me on the head. Come on then, he says. Time to party!

Everyone is here. The patio and the little lawn in the garden is full of friends. Dad is standing by the barbecue. Sausages stacked by his side are piled high from a plate on the ground, to his shoulders. He slips them off the top one by one, steadily not to tip the tower over. Mam is standing next to him, slicing hot-dog buns open, sticking a finger in each crease to open them, sticking her tongue in Dad's ear in between each bun slice. Baby is being held against his will by Sandy, they shower each other in unwanted sand and sugar. Sandy sees me and smiles, sees Green and falls into a heap on the ground. Baby bounces out of his dissolving arms and slides down his forming dune, giggling loudly as he lands on the grass. I pick up Baby and hold him high in the air, shaking him gently and brushing the sand off his bottom. He giggles and coos into my shoulder as I bring him in close to my chest. His little feet rest on my belly like a shelf. Green helps Sandy to his feet as he re-forms, he brushes his hands together to shake off the sugar. Sorry about that, Peach, he says, embarrassed. He's a wriggly little chap! That's okay, Sandy, I say, he's a tough guy. Thank you for holding him. He can't go too near the barbecue, he's melted a couple of times, Mam is worried he'll stretch out and be too tall, I say, grimacing at Dad as he passes Mam a cooked sausage in his mouth. The three of us stand and stare at them. Green puts his hand over Baby's eyes. So what's the special occasion? And where did you get all this meat from? Did you rob a sausage factory? asks Sandy, bemused, but eyes still fixed on Mam and Dad's licking tongues. I didn't prepare an excuse for all this. I shut my eyes and lift my face to the sun. I guess there is no special reason, I say, shrugging my shoulders and hoping I seem nonchalant. Just a beautiful day to share with good people. I smile and kiss Baby's warm squidgy head, warming in the sunshine. Green puts his arm around me, kisses the top of my head. And for the first time since that agonising night I feel all right. All right. And if this bump never goes, if I roll around for the rest of my life, I can be proud of the fighting. The fight. The fast violence that came and went and rocked but just for a moment. Rocked but did not ruin. Sandy is saying something but I am lost in my bliss. He waves and wanders across the lawn to speak to Mr Custard who is containing himself in a plastic picnic chair. He is glossy and bright in the sunlight, radiant and rapidly hardening. He looks in my direction over his shades and waves. He looks from side to side mimicking suspicion, looks back at me, shrugs and smiles widely. He points a blobby finger at the barbecue and winks. He quickly slips his shades back on as Sandy approaches him. What was all that about? asks Green. I'm not sure, I say. But I am. Of course I do. He knows. And oh! Who else? How obvious? Baby wobbles in my shaking arms. What's wrong? asks Green, worriedly. Here, he says, gesturing to the bench on the patio. Let's sit down. Here, I'll take Baby for a bit. He throws Baby high in the sky and catches him as he falls back down to earth and sits him on the bough of his shoulders. I sit on the bench and put my hand on my forehead. I'm okay, I say, really. Just a little bit weak. I probably just need something to eat. I can help you out with that, shouts Dad from the barbecue. He finishes filling Hair Netty's plate with sausages and oddly shaped charred bits of meat and slips a big sausage into a sliced bun. He smears mustard on the sausage and hands it to Green's outstretched hand. Here you go, he shouts, fresh and juicy! You just wait, Peach, you're going to love it! Mam turns to watch me as Green hands me the plate. Suddenly silence. All voices stop. Somebody turns off music that I hadn't noticed was playing. Until now. The silence. Silence. Springtime has stopped. Aching silence. I look around the garden. All faces, serious and stunned faces, stare at me. Mam and Dad's eyes boggle bigger bulging. Spud and Trunk turn, midarm-wrestle, mouths dropping, gaping open. Mr Custard has lifted his shades up, they are resting on and slowly sinking into his forehead, his little eyes are fixed on me (until they gloop off his face). I can't see Hair Netty's expression through her greasy mop but she is turned in my direction. Baby is obliviously sucking Green's twigs. Green is staring intently at me. He is gently nodding, sheer delight shines from his eyes, his smile is wide, he is mouthing the words, willing me to take a big BITE.

I close my eyes. Open my mouth wide. Brace myself for the memory of that night. Mouth doused in vicious viscous unctuosity. Atrocity. Jarring charring. Sharp. And then. Soft. What's this? Not the sickening tough mesh of raw flesh and clinging flaps of sinew and membrane. Not the thick choking gristle. Not the cloying clots of grease. Not the acidic taste of raw rotten meat. I chew slowly, savouring the taste, the texture, the hot melting meat, the light seasoning of pepper and sage? Is that sage? I swallow.

I open my eyes to smiles. Cheering. Laughing. Clapping. Mam dabs away a joyful trickling tear. We knew you could do it, Peach! shouts Dad proudly. I smile. I am so confused. Green bends to kiss me on the forehead, wipes the corner of my mouth gently with his thumb. Mustard, he says. I feel my face get red and rosy.

The music restarts and someone cranks it LOUD. Everyone gathers around the barbecue. Plates are stacked with sausages, random rounds of meat, bread rolls, Spud shaves a little for accompanying fried potatoes. Stuffing faces. Stuff. Slurping. Licking. Burping. Swallowing whole. I watch them all devour my demon and I join in. And the drinks flow. Eating. Dancing. Laughing. Sunshine. Until the sun goes down. Mam throws up in the hedge. Trunk and Spud are rolling around on a picnic blanket on the lawn. Dad lets Baby lick the froth off his beer. Mr Custard is cold-set in the shade still wearing sunglasses singing sea shanties with Sandy as Hair Netty squeaks along.

I am perched on Green's log lap, my face nestled in his neck by the glowing coals of the dying barbecue. Green pokes the coal with his little finger, stokes a little fire. Why did you do it? he asks me, gently. His quiet question unquiets me. I didn't have a choice, I say, plainly. I can't, I won't lie to Green. He knows now, I must be honest. What do you mean, Peach?

Of course you had a choice. If you really didn't want to eat meat, you didn't have to, he says, earnestly. But I know you find it difficult with your mam and dad constantly going on about you being vegetarian. Oh, I say, repacking my murderous secret and putting it on the back shelf of my mind. You liked it, didn't you, he says, he gives my big, meat-filled belly a little squeeze. He is grinning. I give him a kiss. It didn't taste as bad as I thought it would. I sigh. I am contented in his arms. I feel the trauma and tension of the last few days fall away like an old dry scab.

A Little Thought

Bathed in sweat. I can't sleep. I haven't slept. Shivers creep, have crept all night long along my ever-swelling belly skin. Soft and spongy now. Perhaps ready to drop off. I want to go swimming before I see the doctor. Shower and wash off any residual guilt guts gore association.

Final Pieces, Final Peace

Thick slick. Blood bleeds into the water, colour changes copper. I run my fingers through it like lengths of silky hair. I tread, I tread. I reach between my legs and touch until I find the final thread. I tread. The fine fibre I fumble to find with thick fingers, feeling through viscous liquid leaking out, leaking in. Treading still, I dread, I tug the thread. I scream I screech, it pierces the peace of the pool. Shrieks shoot across the water, bounce off the walls and throw down the sound of pain. Cathartic cries dive into the water, creating curling waves that wash high up over my head and push me under. I whirl in the water I twirl as I pull the thread stitches uncurl fixed flesh unfurls. Rolling, reeling, pain passes. I unravel fast. Cold chemical water cleanses my cut my cunt. Past the point.

My eyes take time to see in the liquid light. My arms lift loosely above my head. I raise my eyes to see the thread floating away. I reach for it but it rushes away in a ripple. And as I reach out to the ripple I rip.

Rip ripping split rip ripe raw. I split from the slit between my legs. The slit the split that hasn't healed. Wet flesh tears, strips away. Orange fuzz and flesh floats in front of my eyes. I am stunned I am shocked I am stuck I am fucked. Hush shush water rushes buzzes hums pushes in against my eardrums. Silence sucks at what is left of my skin. I pull away from the pressure that pushes against my static chest. I push against the impenetrable wall of water with limp limbs to feel the split between my legs. A gap, a gaping gash. As I push my fingers in, I feel a hard sharp shard. I run my fingers over it. There are cracks, there are crevices, rough ridges running deep. The shard is a stone, wedged inside me. A pit sitting snug in the pit of my stomach. It is stuck still to the edges where the flesh has fallen away. Soaking soft flesh. My flesh. My stone. My seed.

I bleed. The murky brown water turns vibrant red. The monstrous taste of metal and meat mingles with the repugnant taste of rotten fruit, pushes past my gritted teeth, coats my tongue, coats my throat. My lungs shiver, flutter, stop, splutter, stop spluttering, stopped up with the corrupt water. I push to propel myself with weak arms, disgust drives me forward but the water seeps into my spongy skin until I am saturated. I seem to be sinking. I push, I push, pressure pushes me back, I push and push but my skin is like wet creasing cardboard, my arms are fat rolls of soaked tissue, they bend, they break away from my shoulder sockets. The tearing is slow. Flaccid fleshy fingers wave goodbye as they dissolve disintegrate minuscule molecules melt away.

I sprout red ribbons from my shoulder blades, thin wings, writhing and rolling around my torso, shrouds of frayed red sheets. I shut my eyes against the firm flow of violent red. Black eyes blind.

In the blackness I think about the loss of my limbs. I won't touch I won't feel. Goodbye Green. I cannot wave goodbye. Baby, Baby I cannot cradle. If these wings could fly I would fly to you. They can't. They are weak. They leak. The blood has flown.

Liquid outside, liquid in, back to sticky, back to thick fluid sugar-syrup-tasting juice, tastes like fruit rotten. The bad seed the bad fruit soft sour like road kill rotten in a hedge the fuzz the fur, I buzz with final breaths.

Against the black of my eyelids I see nothing but shadows swimming towards me, swimming away. The slit splits further across my belly. I feel the flesh fall. I fall with it. My legs are eroding.

Suddenly I am flushed with fear. I can't cry, my face is melting. My lips open, my eyes won't open. The blessing will be that I can't see the bottom. What have I learned who have I hurt is this it. Nothing but flesh. Was this all for nothing other than the craving of fresh flesh. Senseless flesh. I am nothing but solid stone, alone, sinking, how can I still think when my face is all gone. What will they find at the bottom, will they know I was here because I carved you into my heart and I think this heavy rock, this stone, this seed will still have the shape of you inside, look closely at the cracks, slide into the crevices, you will see. I can't I can't I won't grow in this stagnant pond, this soiled water, this stinking pit, this is it, I can't I won't grow, I can't hold I can't hold I feel I am close I feel the scratch and scrape the stone on the ceramic tiles the stone the stone the stone on stone, I can't grow I won't hold I can't hold. I can't grow. I can't hold any soul.

In this pit I will sit. In this pit I will sit. In this. In this. Pit.

Acknowledgements

Thank you to Todd McEwen and Lucy Ellmann for their invaluable guidance, patience and enthusiasm. Thanks to Alexandra, Angelique and Maddy at Bloomsbury for believing in *Peach* and for encouraging me to remain creatively free.

I would like to thank my mother, Christine, my father, Robert, and my sister, Kate, for their love and support.

I would like to thank my writing group, the *Woolpackers* for inspiring me to continue writing *Peach*, for supporting me through the excruciating process of finishing a piece started so long ago. I am enthralled by your talent and dedication. In particular, I would like to thank Tim for his belief, Anna for her persistence and Harry for his insight.

Thank you to Tom, a real-life Green.

I would like to acknowledge the influence and brilliance of Gertrude Stein, James Joyce, Dylan Thomas, Kate Bush and Justin Vernon. I am stunned by the beauty of your words.

A Note on the Type

The text of this book is set in Bembo, which was first used in 1495 by the Venetian printer Aldus Manutius for Cardinal Bembo's *De Aetna*. The original types were cut for Manutius by Francesco Griffo. Bembo was one of the types used by Claude Garamond (1480–1561) as a model for his Romain de l'Université, and so it was a forerunner of what became the standard European type for the following two centuries. Its modern form follows the original types and was designed for Monotype in 1929.